Planning for Murder

Also published in Large Print
by Anne Morice:

Fatal Charm
Treble Exposure
Publish and Be Killed
Dead on Cue
Death and the Dutiful Daughter

Planning for Murder

Anne Morice

G.K.HALL &CO.
Boston, Massachusetts
1991

Published in Large Print by arrangement with
St. Martin's Press, Inc.

G.K. Hall Large Print Book Series.

Set in 16 pt. Plantin.

Library of Congress Cataloging-in-Publication Data

Morice, Anne.
    Planning for murder / Anne Morice.
      p.   cm.—(G.K. Hall large print book series) (Nightingale
series)
   ISBN 0-8161-5246-2
   1. Large type books. I. Title.
PR6063.O743P55   1991b
823'.914—dc20   91-18695

One

1

'Things appear to have got into a bit of a mess since I last descended on you,' Miranda Jones observed, casting a disapproving eye round her father's studio on the Wednesday before Easter. 'It's lucky I decided to come for the whole week.'

Miranda, who was then in her second year at a London ballet school and shared a flat in Battersea with her friends, Lucy and Mark, spent most Saturday and Sunday nights, as well as the major part of her summer vacation, at East End House in West Sussex, where she had been born and, after a fashion, brought up. There were times, especially during the winter, when she would have chosen to be elsewhere, but she had a strong sense of responsibility as well as affection for her father, Billy Jones, who was an architect and on the reclusive side. And, to be absolutely honest, of late West

Sussex offered other inducements for frequent visits, which for the time being Miranda chose to keep to herself.

Miranda's somewhat exceptional filial attitude dated from her early childhood when her mother, discovering herself to be unfitted for marriage and motherhood and, most of all, Billy's reclusiveness, had thrown in the towel and departed to take up residence with a woman friend in Provence. This domestic upheaval had made a lasting impression on Miranda. She had grown up to be a well-adjusted and self-reliant young person and, aware of these virtues herself, attributed them largely to never having needed to play off one parent against the other in order to gain the attention of both, and never having been ruled by the whims of an older and, she had reason to believe, sillier woman.

As a result, her main sense of responsibility towards her father lay in her determination to prevent his making the same mistake twice, for she had small faith in his judgement in such matters, allied to plenty in her own to recognise disaster when she saw it looming and to nip it in the bud.

'I trust you are speaking metaphorically,' he told her.

'What does that mean?'

'That I could bear it better if your purpose is to bully me about taking more exercise, getting my hair cut, paying the bills promptly and cutting down on alcohol. What I should find objectionable is any plan you may have for spring cleaning the house and tidying up all my possessions, so that I have to spend three weeks looking for them when you have gone.'

'I'll bear it in mind,' Miranda assured him, not yet ready to commit herself. In fact, her mission this time, with a whole week set aside for it, did not belong to either category, although closer to the first than the second. It had come to her ears that he had now got himself into a pickle of a different nature, to the point where even his staunch friend and powerful ally, Avril Meyer, was beginning to look askance, while in different circles words such as bribery and corruption were being freely bandied about.

Her informant in this, as in many other matters of local interest, was Martha Kershaw, another old friend of Billy's and in many ways a more perceptive one. There was nothing at all powerful about Martha, who was a middle-aged spinster of small means, no looks and very few opinions which she considered to be worth airing in public. For all these reasons she was largely ignored by members of West Sussex 'society', although not by Avril, who recognised her true worth and, compared with herself, intellectual superiority.

She was also popular with the younger generation, a fact which some of their parents found odd, if not incomprehensible, although to Martha herself the reason seemed plain enough. There was shrewdness in this, but no vanity for, as only a few days earlier she had attempted to explain to Avril, 'I think they see me as one of the few survivors of a dying breed and therefore in need of protection.'

'Oh, they do, do they? Personally, I'd always thought of you as the original ostrich. What breed do they consider yours to be?'

'The maiden aunt, as portrayed in those Victorian novels some of them read in their teens. She was not always an agreeable woman, but she occupied a unique place in the family circle and they feel about me rather as they would if they discovered that Father Christmas really does come down the chimney with a sack of presents on Christmas Eve.'

'Well, I expect you're right, as usual, Martha. I'm afraid they're more likely to see me as Lady Catherine de Burgh.'

'I shouldn't be at all surprised.'

'Right, so now we've got that sorted out, let's go back to what led up to it. You were saying you'd written to Miranda to ask her to get down off her points for a few days to see if she can find out what her old man's up to and, if possible, put a stop to it.'

'Not in those precise words. In fact, I've brought the letter with me for you to cast an eye over before I send it. You can give me your opinion.'

'Oh, always ready with that, as you know. Let's have a dekko.'

Martha had written as follows:

Dearest Miranda,

Such a lovely surprise to hear your voice on the telephone last night and good news that you plan to come down for Easter. I expect I sounded a bit gormless, but, as usual, only found the right words to express what was in my mind after you had rung off, so I will now try to explain.

5

Without wishing to cause you the slightest alarm, I do think it might be a good idea if you were to stay on for an extra day or two, as some of us are beginning to feel a tiny bit worried about your father. He's not in the least unwell, I hasten to assure you. In fact, I've rarely seen him so active (what you would call 'jumping about') as he's been for the past few weeks. In a funny way, that's what I find the most worrying side of it because it's so unlike him, you know, and I can't help being afraid that all this enthusiasm for the job he's now working on is going to blow up in his face.

To be as brief as possible, it concerns a huge development scheme, whereby Mr Waddington who, as you'll remember, moved into Uppfield Court years ago when the old man died, means to use about four hundred acres of the land to create a sort of 'new town', complete with shopping precinct, sports centre and cinema.

As you may imagine, when this was first mooted none of us took it seriously. We'd always assumed in a vague sort of way that it was scheduled as agricultural land and that no local council would ever be empowered to grant building permission on anything like such a scale and ruin the environment for what strikes most people as such a totally unnecessary purpose.

However, it now turns out that, what with all the new Common Market rules and one thing and another, farming is not nearly such a profitable game as it used to be and landowners like Mr Waddington are having to cut down on their labour force and turn what used to be arable and cereal producing land into things like golf courses and camping sites, which I suppose is what you might describe as the thin end of the wedge. Of course, there's bound to be a public outcry before they can push it through, but we hear that he is working hand in glove with some powerful great consortium, if that's the right word, who are prepared to spend whatever it takes to fight their case through the courts and a few million more putting up their nasty housing estates and so-called amenities.

And so now, dearest Miranda, you must be asking yourself why, since the battle appears to be three-quarters lost, I should be boring you with this sad tale at all, when you'll be hearing about it *ad nauseam* as soon as you set foot here. The answer, I'm sorry to say, is that I felt I ought to warn you that your father is taking quite the opposite line from the rest of us and, incredible as it must sound, is quite in favour of the scheme. You will say, of course, that he is just being his usual perverse self and not to be taken seriously, but I have to tell you that it goes a good deal deeper than that. He has accepted Mr Waddington's offer to become overall consultant architect and to produce his own designs for the showpiece area, which is to be a grand sort of residential estate and golf course.

He is most unwilling to discuss it openly and, as you may imagine, gets very cross and stubborn whenever the subject comes up. I did steel myself to ask him whether he had told you about all this and, having got the distinct impression that he had not, thought I ought to warn you that you'll be plunged into rather deep waters and, since we're all relying on you to bring

him to his senses, to be prepared.
Looking forward so much to seeing
you,

Love Martha

'Masterly! You've excelled yourself,' Avril said, impressed as always by anyone with the facility to string half a dozen sentences together. 'I just hope you haven't stated the case so well that it will put her off coming at all.'

'Oh, you can't be serious, Avril! I certainly shan't post it if you are.'

'Don't get excited, it's only my joke. Miranda's as tough as old boots and not likely to be intimidated by the prospect of a blazing row with her old man. Rather the reverse, in my opinion. In the meantime, Martha, it's given me an idea. Remember my telling you about the Gillfords?'

'Those friends of yours who've bought a house over towards Lewes?'

'Not bought, only rented, and not exactly friends, either. Janet and I were mates for a time in our salad days, but I've never met her husband and I haven't seen her for donkey's years. The husband, Geoffrey Gillford, worked for the British Council, so they've been living abroad mostly. Anyway, he's retired now and she wrote to say how lovely it was that we were practically going to be next-door neighbours and the point is they've got a grown-up son.'

'I can understand why a distance of twelve or fifteen miles might seem like practically next door to someone who was used to the wide open spaces, but would you mind explaining why the grown-up son is the point?'

'Ah well, you see, he lives in London and only comes down here at weekends, just like Miranda, so I thought that would make a bond, to kick off with.'

'My dear Avril, don't tell me you're going in for matchmaking now?'

'No, certainly not. Well, only as a sideline, but this is something much more subtle. You see, I thought of inviting them all over for lunch on Easter Sunday. I'm not sure yet whether Robert will be back from America by then, but, much as I can't wait to see him, it would really suit my plans better if he weren't, because then I should be in a stronger position to throw myself on Miranda's mercy.'

'Am I to take it that you intend to invite her and Billy to this schoolgirl reunion?'

'Exactly, Martha! And you too, if you'll come. I thought it would be a clever way of prising Billy out of his shell. The Gillfords are too new to the neighbourhood to have heard about the Waddington disaster and too far away for it to affect them, even if it does go through. All the same, Billy probably wouldn't come on his own, especially if he thought there was any chance of Robert being here. He's scared silly of him at the best of times, as you know. On the other hand, if I've already got Miranda sewn up he won't have much of a leg to stand on.'

'Well, it might work, I suppose. As you say, there'll be no reproachful looks from these Gillfords and I feel convinced that is what is getting him down. Having manoeuvred himself into this silly situation, mainly through vagueness, I shouldn't wonder, I think he could have borne up better in a climate of open hostility. It's the way all his old friends are now treating him as though he had some unmentionable disease which must be so trying.'

'Entirely his own fault, of course, but I think you're right and we shall have a much better chance of knocking the stuffing out of him if we try treating him as a normal human being. The presence of strangers will be a great help there and we can rely on

Miranda to deliver the knock-out blow when the time comes. I just hope he'll deign to step down from his high horse and accept my invitation.'

'I don't see why not,' Martha said, 'since it's well known that he'd walk barefoot to the ends of the earth for you any time you decided to ask him.'

'A slight exaggeration. But we have known each other for a very long time and just because he's become an obstinate, anti-social, pigheaded old pain in the neck is no reason why we shouldn't still be good friends.' Avril made rapid notes in her diary, deposited that volume in her extremely chic handbag, shutting it with the finality of a mantrap.

2

The invitation to lunch on Easter Sunday was accepted on behalf of all three Gillfords, as well as by Billy Jones and Miranda, but Robert Meyer found himself unable to return from his business trip to Atlanta in time for it.

On hearing this, Martha did her feeble best to back out too, using the excuse that it would make an awkward number at the table, but Avril would have none of it.

'Sorry, Martha, but that won't do. In the first place, you know perfectly well that I don't give a damn about such things and, in the second, I've already asked Tubby Wiseman, which will make the numbers dead even again. So you'll have to think of a better excuse than that.'

'Which, unfortunately, I was unable to do and she wouldn't have liked the true one any better,' Martha explained later that day to Miranda, who had called round to ask for the use of her telephone, in order to report that theirs was out of order.

'And what is the true explanation?' she asked, having dealt with this matter in her usual competent fashion.

'That I'm so hopelessly conscious of my own social inadequacies that the prospect of being flung among strangers throws me into a near panic. No good trying to explain that to Avril. Her imagination simply wouldn't be able to encompass such a thing. You don't think, Miranda dear, that your father might have played some little trick with the telephone which has put it out of order?'

'No, not this time. I agree that he's capable of it. He's almost as neurotically anti-social as you are, but he wouldn't sink as low as that. For one thing, when I'm here to act as switchboard operator and intercept all incoming calls I have instructions to say he's busy just now. Whereas, if I'm not here, someone might be phoning to tell him that I'd been carted off to the hospital with two broken legs and then he'd have it on his conscience for ever after.'

'Yes, I expect that's true,' Martha admitted, somewhat daunted, as usual, by Miranda's realistic attitude to life. 'I expect you understand him perfectly.'

'Well, enough to badger him into escorting me to Avril's lunch party, I hope. Going out into the world and meeting new people is just what he needs at the moment, in my opinion. He's been stuck at home, brooding over his injuries for far too long, by the look of him. And, if it's of any interest, I'm thankful Avril wouldn't let you off, either. One of my main inducements was that you'd be among the company.'

This, despite the suspicion that she herself was now being managed and manipulated, was too gratifying to be resisted and Martha said no more about backing out.

──Two────────────

1

Janet Gillford also had to break down opposition before composing her letter of acceptance, although, since the main rebel was her husband, she was able, through long experience, to out-manoeuvre him with a single, well-aimed stroke.

There was no malice or selfishness behind this, for it was as much for his own benefit as hers. The fact was, she regarded him as a near-genius, as well as one of the noblest and most handsome of men and, as a result, ill equipped to recognise or protect his own interests. So, if she was sometimes compelled to resort to tricks and subterfuge, it was simply because, being made of inferior stuff, these were the only weapons with which Nature had provided her for the job.

Janet was his second wife and junior to him by fifteen years. Her predecessor had been a Canadian divorcée named Jennifer, whom Geoffrey had met on a Union Castle liner early in his career and on his way to his first posting outside Europe. He had chosen to travel by sea in order to spend those three weeks working through a pile of documents and briefings relating to the African country which was to be his home for the next five years. As things turned out, however, he could have saved himself the trouble, for by the time he went ashore he had collected about as much information on the subject as could have been acquired between meals on an eight-hour flight.

Jennifer at that time was in her early twenties, pretty and on the plump side, with flaxen hair and china-blue eyes. She also had a sweet expression, which appeared truly to reflect her nature, for never once during the whole voyage did Geoffrey hear her utter an unkind word about another passenger, or the husband who had obviously treated her so badly, or indeed about anyone at all.

She was also engagingly frank in admitting her deficiencies in knowledge and understanding of the world, forever begging for enlightenment, so that within a few days it had become a duty, as well as a pleasure to take on this task. On their last evening at sea they became engaged and the wedding took place a few weeks later, with the High Commissioner giving the bride away.

The marriage lasted for less than two

years, however. Long before then Jennifer had grown bored by Geoffrey's attempts to fill the gaps in her education and still more so by the restricted social life within the small European community in their corner of darkest Africa. The climate did not suit her either and when their second hot season was approaching she departed on an extended visit to her family in Canada.

It had been arranged that they would reunite in London, when he came on home leave later in the year, but by the time he arrived she had found someone else to supervise her education and soon afterwards proceedings were put in hand for divorce.

For the next ten years he became a bachelor again. At the end of them, during a stint at headquarters, which he disliked intensely, he had met and married Janet, then a junior secretary who had rapidly become well versed in taking dictation and transferring it, in slightly more readable form to the written page—one of the many talents which she was later able to develop and adapt to the social and domestic environment.

Since then and for the remainder of his working life hardly a week had gone by which did not give him reason to congratulate himself on the wisdom of his choice. Always putting his wishes first without his needing to express them, Janet had gone out of her way to be gracious and hospitable to those who were important or useful to him, while protecting him, as though by instinct, from bores and nonentities, particularly the chummy kind who were liable to address him as Geoff, and carefully scripting her own conversation to bring out the best in his. He could not doubt that some small part of his success, at least, had been due to her.

The same rules and precepts had also governed their private and domestic lives. Unlike many of his friends, it was for him to make the decisions and for her to carry them out, which she had invariably managed to do without criticism or argument.

A dramatic example of this had occurred when Geoffrey walked in one morning after a round of golf and announced out of the blue that he intended to retire the following year when he would be sixty, the earliest date on which he would become eligible for a pension. Janet had looked surprised, as well she might, and a little disappointed too, which was also to be expected, seeing that this would mean sacrificing at least one third of the income which would have been his, had he stuck to his original intention of staying on in the job for the extra five years.

This bombshell, which failed to detonate a single objection from Janet, had been dropped during their last home leave, part of which had been spent in a furnished cottage near the South Coast and later the same day, when she had made some mental adjustments, she asked Geoffrey whether it was being back in England again that had persuaded him to change course. He told her that it was and that, furthermore, this particular part of the country attracted him more than any other he had seen. So near the sea, so conveniently situated for London and yet so unspoilt; how could they do better than to make it their permanent home?

As usual, Janet had fallen in with his demands and so it was that a year and a half later they had taken up temporary residence at Dormer Hill, midway between Newhaven and Lewes.

Now that he was retired, however, and with leisure at last to work on the autobiography which was to be the culmination of his career or, better still, the launching pad for a brand new one in literature, a little flexibility was required from Janet and was not always forthcoming.

There had been, for example, his insistence that the single south-facing, ground-floor room in their rented house should be set aside as his library, which no one could enter without his permission and that he should retire there every morning after breakfast, not to be disturbed on any pretext whatever until lunch time. House-hunting must be reserved for afternoons.

The trouble was that after only ten days of this regime he had come to regret it and began searching for dignified excuses to break out. Infinite leisure, unexpectedly enough, was turning out to be self-defeating. Ideas came tumbling into his head, just as he had always promised himself they would, but all too often the words to express them eluded him. The fact that he could afford to wait for another two or three hours, or even days, before they began to flow only compounded the evil. There were times when he could have strangled Janet for not interrupting him, especially when he heard the telephone ringing in the adjoining room and sprang up, with groans and curses, only to be forestalled by the sound of his thoughtful wife's hushed voice answering it.

All this was well understood by Janet, for whom the situation was equally frustrating. Viewing houses during afternoons only, for instance, was usually a waste of time, since anything attractive which came on the market at nine in the morning was more than likely to be labelled 'Under Offer' by midday. However, she had no intention of relaxing her vigilance, for she did not wish to spend her twilight years listening to complaints about the autobiography which had never been completed, owing to the pressures of domestic life. Furthermore, she had become reconciled over the years to the fact that even the most brilliant mind had its childish side and that the more relentlessly she co-operated in preserving his isolation the faster it would lose its appeal for him. In months, if not weeks, he would turn against the idea of writing his memoirs, because to do so would mean betraying too many official secrets, or some such face-saving excuse, would take up golf again and life would return to normal.

The same policy was responsible for her bland acceptance of his decision not to wear a formal suit for Avril's luncheon party. She listened unmoved while he expatiated at some length on the vulgar pretensions of those who dressed themselves up as though for a board meeting to go out to lunch with friends in the country and that flannel trousers and a tweed jacket would suit the purpose very well. At the end of it, having applauded this stand, she said she would just telephone Avril about it, in case their host, should he be present and so misguided as to appear in a collar and tie, should be made to appear vulgar and pretentious by one of his guests. Geoffrey said that she could do as she liked, it was all one to him and two hours later, when he came downstairs to take his place behind the wheel, he had on a blue shirt and tie, which toned to perfection with his best tweed suit, explaining that both his jackets had missing buttons.

Janet did not resort to these tactics where her son's wardrobe was concerned because, on the whole, she preferred him to look like a student from the Poly, which he was, rather than an advertising agent, which he was hoping to become.

After all, Robert Meyer was not among the party, but neither was the tweed suit wasted because Miranda had also prevailed upon her escort to smarten up for the occasion, although using a more direct and hectoring approach than Janet. On the other hand, being better versed in contemporary fashions than Janet, she had needed only one glance at Anthony Gillford's tatty woollen shirt and leather-patched jacket to recognise a would-be ad man or film director.

However, Theodore Wiseman, who had been brought in at the last minute, possessed the proportions and self-assurance to have stopped a wider gap than this. He was a good-humoured, urbane man in his fifties, a bachelor who enjoyed the company of women, perhaps all the more because he did not have to live with them. He was also Chief Superintendent of the local division of the CID, but no reference was made to this in the introductions, since on social occasions he preferred to sail under the flag of plain Mr Wiseman, or Tubby to his friends.

Martha, with Billy Jones and Miranda, who had been bidden to come early, were in fact the last to arrive, for which Miranda was the culprit. Having been the last one to use her father's car, she had thoughtfully and efficiently backed it into the garage and then, after checking that there was enough petrol in the tank to get them to Avril's house and back, had put the keys away in an obvious place. Unfortunately, when the time came to take them out again she had forgotten where that was.

It was the kind of thing that frequently happened to Miranda because, as a reaction to her father's slapdash ways, she had developed an obsession about neatness and order and was forever putting things away in their right place. The trouble was that what had seemed right on Friday evening had invariably become wrong by Sunday morning.

This phenomenon was the source of some amusement to her father, who was constantly being plagued to clear up the mess and clutter with which he surrounded himself, despite the fact that he never had the slightest difficulty in laying his hands on a single object whenever it was needed.

On this occasion he had stood by indifferently for twenty minutes, watching her tip out the contents of two handbags, pull open drawers and search in pockets to no avail and then said, 'Before you create any more work for yourself it might be a good idea to telephone Martha. You could just be in time to catch her before she leaves.'

'Why? What's Martha got to do with it?'

'Everything. She can come here and pick us up on her way.'

'Except that it's not on her way.'

'No matter. Martha won't mind.'

'But that'll make us all late.'

'Not half as late as you and I are going to be if we have to walk, or wait for Lubbocks to send a taxi to collect us.'

'Oh, very well, but you see to it, will you? She'll probably take it better from you.'

While he was doing so a last, faint hope leapt into her mind and sent her racing out to the garage. The keys were in the ignition, where she had undoubtedly left them, but since, however logical, this was hardly the most sensible place in the world, she pocketed them and decided not to refer to the matter again until interest in the subject had died down.

2

'How's the house-hunting getting on?' Avril asked at lunch. 'Any luck yet?'

'I'm afraid we haven't been able to spend as much time on it as we'd hoped,' Janet told her. 'It's taking us a while to get our bearings, if you know what I mean.'

Avril, who had been listening to Geoffrey before lunch, thought she could guess what Janet meant and she said, 'Well, there's no great hurry, I suppose? You seem to be pretty comfortable where you are, by the sound of it. How long have you got it for?'

'That's what we're not sure about, unfortunately. I realise this must sound strange, but the house only came into our hands by a fluke and we could be moving out again in three months' time.'

The others appeared to be rather nonplussed by this statement and Anthony weighed in as interpreter. 'What my mother is trying to say is that we're not tenants in the regular sense, more like paying caretakers.'

'Well, I must say that doesn't sound like a very good bargain. What do you think, Tubby?'

'I agree, but I think I can see how it came about this time. Would I be right in saying, Mrs Gillford, that the house is called Dormer Hill?'

'Quite right. You know of it?'

'Never been inside, but I've met the owner. Farmer called James Crossman. You know the chap I mean, Avril?'

'I know one of that name, but he doesn't

live in anything called Dormer Hill. He owns that big farm just the other side of Redlye.'

'Yes, but he bought Dormer about six months ago as a wedding present for his son. Next thing was the engagement was broken off and the house was up for letting.'

'Didn't the girl like it?' Billy asked, rousing himself from the torpor which had set in before lunch, while having to sit through a dissertation from Geoffrey Gillford on the problems of the Middle East and how they should be solved.

'More likely, she didn't fancy living within a few miles of her father-in-law,' Martha said. 'So far as I know—I've never set eyes on him—he has the reputation of being a very glum old party.'

Janet shook her head. 'No, it wasn't for either of those reasons, something much more dramatic. A few weeks after the engagement was announced she fell in love with someone else. A shame, really. Rupert Crossman is such a nice boy. According to Mr Crossman this someone else is a good bit older than she is and very, very rich.'

'So perhaps Billy was on the right track, after all. In the meantime, now that your house is no longer required by the happy couple, why not make an offer for it?'

'Not nearly large enough, for one thing,' Geoffrey said, jumping in before his wife could answer. 'We need a decent-sized library, for a start.'

'Oh, you could build one on, I expect. There wouldn't be any problem about planning permission, so long as it couldn't be seen from the road.'

'The real problem,' Janet explained, 'is that Mr Crossman has no intention of selling it. He is determined that his beloved son shall have it when he does marry and, now that the first candidate has dropped out, it is simply a question of waiting for the next one to come along. Having seen the young man, I shouldn't think he'd have long to wait.'

'Attractive lad, is he?'

'Oh, very, and oozing with charm.'

'There now,' Avril said, casting a speculative eye at Miranda who seemed to her to be unusually silent and whom, until then, she had been hoping to pair off with young Mr Gillford. 'Well, how about it, Billy? You're more likely than the rest of us to be up to date on these matters. Any snips likely to be coming on the market round here?'

'Well, there's always the Court, of course, providing the Council let us have our way about it. That should be available in six months or so. Lot to be done to it, of course.'

There had been a sharp intake of breath on the part of three of those present at this allusion to Uppfield Court, it being the property of the notorious Mr Waddington. However, their reaction had been foreseen by Billy, who was growing tired of being treated like a rebellious adolescent, more likely to grow out of this tiresome phase all the quicker if everyone treated him with tact and ignored its existence.

Oblivious of this tangled web, Janet said, 'I'm afraid it sounds a bit too grand for us. We only need what the agents describe as four to five bed and three recep.'

'No matter. That could easily be arranged.'

'By razing three-quarters of it to the ground, presumably?' Tubby enquired, also unaware of the taboo. 'It's years since I went to Uppfield, but I'd judge it to have all of twenty rooms.'

'Very true, but the plan is to divide it up into separate, self-contained units. The exact number has still to be decided.'

'Sounds quite promising,' Janet said, evidently warming to the idea of living in a Court. 'Who is one supposed to get in touch with about it?'

'The owner is a man called Waddington. I could sound him out, if you're really interested.'

'Oh, I'm sure we could do better for you than that,' Avril said, seizing the reins again at this point. 'I don't know about you, Janet, but personally I shouldn't at all fancy being in a place like that, cheek by jowl with other families. Might as well live in a block of flats and have done with it.'

'Although I suppose there might be certain advantages. One wouldn't need to worry so much about burglars getting in, for instance, if one wanted to go away for a few days. What do you say, Anthony? You're looking very thoughtful.'

'Not about the house, which I think sounds a fairly rotten idea. It was the name Waddington that rang a bell. I knew I'd heard it somewhere before and it's just hit me. Didn't you know someone called Waddington in Singapore, Dad? Rather funny if it turned out to be the same bloke.'

'Most unlikely,' his mother said. 'There was never any mention of the man your father knew owning a big house in Sussex. He always appeared to be rather hard up.'

'That could have been before his father died,' Avril told her. 'he made pots of money out of bootlaces or something and in the end he left everything to his son, although the story goes that he had no time at all for him when he was alive. Small world, as they say.'

'Yes, they do,' Geoffrey said, 'but this is hardly an illustration of the point. If the Waddington we knew had had a rich father, we'd have heard about it, whether they got on or not. You can be sure of that.'

Avril, however, was unwilling to be sure of anything which dashed such promising hopes of finding out something discreditable about the past history of Mr Waddington of Uppfield Court.

'Well, I don't see how that proves anything,' she said. 'Maybe he just didn't like boasting about it. What was your friend's first name, by the way, Geoffrey?'

'I'm afraid I can't remember.'

'Neither can I,' Janet said, recognising his tone. 'What a pity.'

Anthony, however, was not a spent force yet. 'I can, though. I never met him, but I remember my father telling me about him and I'd been reading that book about Jim, you know the one I mean?'

'*Captain Jim?*' Tubby suggested.

'Not Captain, no, something else Jim. "Lucky", that's the one, *Lucky Jim,* and the character seemed to fit, in a way, so it sort of stuck in my mind.'

'So there we are,' Avril said, 'point settled. They're not the same man, after all. How disappointing. Ours is called Sam.'

'No need to be downhearted, Sam could be Jim, or Wilfred or Zebedee for that matter,' Billy informed her. 'I happen to know that Sam is short for Samson and was the name of the grandfather who founded the family fortune. One of the more eccentric conditions of Waddington's inheritance was that he should adopt the name as his own, which I may say he was more than ready to do. So for the past eight or ten years he has been Sam, but before that he went under quite a different name, which I am sorry to say I have now forgotten.'

'Surely there is a simpler way of settling the argument,' Tubby said. 'The most distinctive feature of our man is the scar across his forehead, from the bridge of his nose up to his right temple and once seen never forgotten, I'd have thought.'

Janet opened her mouth, but before she could speak Geoffrey stepped in and brushed the whole question aside. 'I am afraid this is really all quite irrelevant. The Waddington I used to know has been dead for years. I heard that he got drunker than usual one night and smashed his car to pieces and himself with it in some remote hole somewhere.'

These remarks were made not in a conversational tone, but as a statement of facts, indicating that there was nothing further to be said on the subject. As though recognising this, a hush descended on the rest of the party and, looking around at the older guests, at Martha nervously pushing the food round on her plate, Avril struggling to find a less contentious subject by giving out the news that the local farmers were becoming seriously worried by the drought and Billy subsiding again into his private dream, it occurred to Tubby that the party could hardly have got off to a less convivial start had Robert been presiding over it himself.

—Three—

1

'When did you hear about that friend of yours, Waddington, being killed in a car crash?' Janet asked her husband at breakfast the following morning. There had been no opportunity to do so before because for some reason which she was unable to identify she had been reluctant to introduce the subject in Anthony's presence and immediately after dinner Geoffrey had taken himself off to the library, where he remained until after she was asleep.

'Oh, years ago,' he replied, looking up from his newspaper. 'Can't remember exactly. I must have mentioned it at the time, though.'

'I don't think so, or I'm sure I would have remembered. Who was it who told you?'

'My dear girl, what an absurd question! It must have been someone we knew in Bangkok or Singapore, I suppose, but I wasn't all that interested, to tell you the truth. Hadn't seen him for years and didn't care much for him when I did.'

'I know that. Funnily enough, it was why I was surprised that you'd kept so quiet about his death.'

'Oh, what nonsense! What's much more likely is that I told you about it at the time and it went in one ear and out the other. It must be all of ten years ago, after all. Have you got anything lined up for us to view this afternoon?'

'Nothing definite. No appointments, that is, and the estate agents are closed today for the Bank Holiday. I thought it might be fun to drive over and take a look at Uppfield Court, the house Mr Jones was telling us about, just to get an idea of whether it would be worth while going into it seriously.'

'Well, as to that, you must do as you please, of course, but I should warn you that you'll be wasting your time. I haven't the faintest intention of pursuing it.'

'Really? Why ever not? I thought it sounded quite suitable.'

'I'm afraid nothing on earth would induce me to live in one part of a house with other people living in other parts, including dogs and children, very likely. Communal life is not my style at all.'

'Oh, but each set of apartments would be entirely self-contained, you know, and big old houses like that always have such thick walls, nothing like the modern blocks of flats.'

'Well, as I say, you must do as you please, if it amuses you. By all means go and have a look at it, but don't delude yourself that I'd ever consider it as a place to end my days.'

Stung as she had rarely been before by his obstinacy and condescension, Janet made up her mind on the spot that she would go and see it and as soon as he had taken himself off to the library she went upstairs to find out if Anthony was still in bed. In fact, he was in the bathroom, where the pop music competed with the sound of running water. This was even better, from her point of view, and she continued on to her bedroom, picked up the telephone and dialled Avril's number. Having thanked her for the wonderful lunch and delightful company of the previous day, she added, as though struck by an afterthought, 'Oh, by the way, Avril, Geoffrey seems quite interested in the idea of our buying part of that big house Mr Jones was telling us about. So, as a first step, I was thinking of driving over there this morning to take a look at the surroundings and so on. I suppose there wouldn't be any chance of your being free to come too?'

'Afraid not, Janet,' Avril replied, not best pleased to hear that her old friend was moving so swiftly into the enemy camp. 'Not a chance, I'm afraid. With Robert away, everything gets thrown on to me, you see, and I've got our bailiff coming here for a consultation this morning. Awfully sorry.'

'Oh, please don't be,' Janet said, the coolness of Avril's response not having escaped her. She had also noticed a certain antagonism towards Mr Jones when this subject was mooted, which made her feel confident that her enquiries would not be reported back and her next move was to look up his number in the directory and ring him up.

However, different rules obtained in the Jones's household and it was Miranda who answered. She explained that her father was at work in his studio, which in fact was where he had spent almost every morning of his life for as long as she could remember and the studio had been built at the furthest end of the garden, for the express purpose of protecting him from the telephone.

'Would you like to leave a message?' she asked. 'I'm afraid there's no guarantee he'll get it until this evening.'

'Oh, I see. Well, in that case, I wonder if you could help me.'

'I will if I can. What did you want to ask him?'

'About that house he was describing to us at lunch yesterday. I find myself with time on my hands for once, and I thought of driving over to take a look at it.'

'Well, why not?'

'The trouble is that I only have the haziest idea of where it is and how to get there. I was hoping your father would be able to give me some directions, but perhaps you could tell me?'

'Yes, of course. If you're coming from the Lewes direction, your best bet would be to go on the Brighton road until you come to a village called Redlye. It's about five miles and then you turn right at the next crossroads, which is signposted to Haywards Heath. After that, it gets a bit complicated, I'm afraid.'

'In that case, would you mind holding on for a second while I find a pencil?'

When she picked up the telephone again Miranda said, 'I have a better idea. Why not meet me at Redlye and we'll drive the rest of the way together? It's only about four miles from there to Uppfield, but it's not signposted and you could go round and round for hours.'

'That's extremely kind of you, Miranda, but are you sure? I mean, it's not much of a holiday for you.'

'Oh, that's okay. I wouldn't half mind having another look at the place myself as it happens, and I've got some . . . er . . . shopping to do anyway, so it's more or less on my route. Would about an hour from now suit you?'

'Yes, that would be splendid.'

'Right. There are two pubs in Redlye, and one of them—can't remember its name—has a big car park and a pond on the other side. It's on the right as you come into the village. I'll be there around ten-thirty.'

Billy Jones turned his head sideways and screwed up his eyes in misery when his daughter marched into the studio ten minutes later. This was his normal reaction to any intrusion during working hours and sometimes out of them as well. However, since she saw that he had been using the white sheet of paper pinned to his drawing board to execute some delicate sketches of human and animal faces, she took it even less seriously than usual. In fact, she regarded it as a sign that the talking to she had given him the previous evening about his current activities was beginning to take effect.

'Don't panic,' she said. 'I've only come to ask if I can borrow the car for a couple of hours.'

'Oh, most certainly,' he assured her, becoming effusive as if at the prospect of a treat in store. 'I shan't need it at all today, so keep it as long as you like. There should be plenty of petrol.'

'Then there'll be plenty left when I get back. I'm only going to do a bit of shopping.'

'Are you really? I imagined all the shops would be shut on Easter Monday.'

'Most of them are, I daresay,' Miranda said, having now recollected this herself, 'but not the garden centre. This is the biggest day of their year and I wanted to get a few plants to take back to London for my window box.'

Instinct told him that all this was a pack of lies and he could not resist saying, as she was leaving, 'Keys turned up safe and sound, then?'

However, Miranda was half way out of

the room by then and pretended not to have heard him.

2

'Shall we go in my car?' Miranda asked. 'It's not as smart as yours, but it does know the way.'

'What a nice idea! Will it be all right to leave this one where it is?'

'Perfectly all right, only you'd better lock it. Funny lot of people in Redlye.'

'I always lock up, even if it's only for five minutes,' Janet said, putting the keys back in her bag. 'Geoffrey insists on it. What's funny about them?'

'Oh, nothing much, really, but they have the reputation of being a bit in-bred and bloody-minded. It probably comes from living in the shadow of the Downs. They have something to be surly about too just now, and one can't tell how the mood may take them.'

'You speak as though they were some isolated, forgotten tribe. It's an oddity I've noticed about Sussex people since we came to live here. Travelling from one village to another is like crossing the frontier into a foreign country. What, in particular, have they to be surly about just now?'

'Well, a lot of them stand to lose their jobs and their homes as well, if this scheme for breaking up the estate goes ahead.'

'Oh dear, that is sad. Although I suppose it will also create new jobs and new homes?'

'That's my father's attitude,' Miranda replied, making it plain that she did not share it.

They had been travelling for some minutes behind a tractor at ten miles an hour along a narrow lane, with cow parsley bordering the hedges on either side, and she explained that they were now inside that part of the estate which had been scheduled for re-development and were approaching the main gates to the house.

'Is there some point where we can get a clear view of it without being seen ourselves?' Janet asked. 'I wouldn't want anyone to think we were snooping around.'

Since snooping around exactly described Janet's purpose, Miranda did not feel any more drawn to her passenger as the minutes went by. However, she controlled her impatience and said, 'It won't really matter if we're seen or not. There may be someone there keeping an eye on things, but it won't be the owner.'

'How do you know?'

'Because, according to my father, he's in Barbados, or wherever it is that people of his kind go at this season.'

'Which kind is that?'

'Oh, with more money than sense, I suppose. I mean, just look around you. If you owned all this, why would you want to be anywhere but here on a day like this?'

'But if he has so much money, why does he have to sell part of the land at all?'

'Don't ask me. Still, that's the way it goes, isn't it? Seems to me it's only the very rich who care so desperately about money, but perhaps it's all that most of them have got.'

'I wouldn't have expected that to apply to Mr Waddington, though. I gather he wasn't what they call a self-made man.'

'No, his father or grandfather made a pile somewhere in the North and the father bought this place when he retired. He was a good landlord, I believe, but neither he nor his wife made any attempt to mix with the locals and after she died he became more reclusive than ever. Most people wouldn't have recognised him if he'd marched in when they were having tea.'

'So it doesn't sound as though being rich brought him much joy. How about this one? Did he get on well with his father?'

'Far from it. No one round here knew of his existence until about ten years ago, when he turned up in our midst. He seems to have taken off for foreign parts as soon as he was old enough and, as far as anyone knows, hadn't been back to this country since. Pity he didn't stay on where he was, most people think. My Dad, who knows him better than most, seems to get on with him all right, but then he's pretty eccentric himself. Oh, good, that beastly tractor's going straight on and here we are at the Lodge,' she added, coming to a stop outside a pair of heavily Gothic-style wrought-iron gates. 'I don't think there's anyone living there at the moment, so we'll have to fend for ourselves.'

'Would you like me to see if I can open them?' Janet asked, without much confidence.

'Yes, please. Then you can shut them again when I've gone through. They won't be locked and they're not as heavy as they look.'

Rather to Janet's annoyance, all this

proved to be true. Although it would have been against her own interests, she wouldn't have minded seeing Miranda getting her comeuppance. Obedience to orders came naturally to her, but not quite so naturally when handed out by a bossy schoolgirl.

'The drive curves round to the right in a moment.' Miranda told her when they were on the move again, 'and then you'll be able to see the house in all its splendour.'

'Splendour' was not really the word, however, for, despite its fine proportions, the house had a desolate and forbidding look about it, as though it had not been occupied for years and would not welcome any change in that state of affairs.

'You seem a bit shattered, Mrs Gillford. Do you think it's hideous?'

'No, not that exactly; very imposing, in fact. It's just that it strikes me as . . . well, rather unfriendly, if that doesn't sound stupid. I can't imagine ever feeling cosy there.'

'Oh, you don't have to worry about that. It'll have been smartened up no end by the time the occupants move in. Besides, people stop noticing what the outside of their house looks like, once they've moved in. Let's go and take a peek through some of the windows.'

'I couldn't be more grateful to you for taking so much trouble and giving up your time like this,' Janet said, as they moved forward again, 'but I really do think I've seen enough to be going on with. I shall be able to tell Geoffrey how splendid the surroundings are and then, if he's still interested, perhaps we can arrange to be taken round by the agent.'

She did not add that her impulse to set forth on this expedition had been due largely to curiosity about the owner of the property and the suspicion that he might be the same Waddington they had known all those years ago in Singapore rather than the house itself and the likelihood of it providing them with a permanent home. The stroke of luck which had sent Miranda as her guide had indeed brought enough information to be going on with, reinforcing the belief that they most likely were one and the same, having learnt more about him during the past ten minutes than could be gleaned from any amount of peering through the windows of an empty house.

'I am sure you have much more interesting things to occupy you than ferrying me around,' she added.

'Oh, that's all right, I rather enjoy looking

at other people's houses. Besides, we have to go on now, whether we like it or not. There's simply no way I could turn round without going up on the bank and probably reversing slap into a tree while I was at it, and that wouldn't please my Dad one bit.'

And even as she spoke they saw a Land-rover approaching from the opposite direction. By inching past each other a foot at a time, and with both sets of nearside wheels up on the grass verge, they managed to complete the operation without damage and, so intent had Miranda been on acquitting herself with honour that she had barely had time to take the smallest interest in the other driver except to notice that it was a man and therefore, in her opinion, unlikely to give an inch if she could be cowed into giving two.

'I wonder who that could have been?' she said, normal curiosity taking over again, once they were on their way.

As it happened, despite having crouched down in her seat, averted her head, and pretended to be invisible, Janet was in a position to enlighten her. However, secrecy being of the essence in this operation, she allowed the question to go by and a minute or so later they came to a stop beside a flight of stone steps, leading up to a columned portico.

'Looks just like something in a television drama, doesn't it? The front door opens into the hall, which is very wide and has two curved staircases which meet in a gallery on first floor level. There's a door at each end of the gallery, leading to another staircase which only serves that side of the house. My father tells me the design was pinched from a house called Monte Cello in Virginia, but anyway you can see how easy it makes it to convert into two or four separate houses.'

'And what will the hall be used for?'

'No idea, but he's got it all worked out, so you'll have to ask him yourself, if you're interested. Come and look at the view from the back.'

'The surroundings are really quite lovely,' Janet remarked, 'with all those trees looking so natural and yet so cunningly grouped. Someone did a first-rate job of landscaping when it was planted out two or three hundred years ago.'

'Too true! People don't worry any longer about what's going to be there in two or three hundred years' time. They just grab what there is now and turn it into money.'

'Since you take such a jaundiced view of the whole scheme, Miranda, I'm rather surprised, although very grateful, of course, that you should have gone to all this trouble to show me round.'

'Oh well, just curiosity, really. It's years since I set foot in the place, so I thought I might as well take a last look. Besides, if it's going to happen, anyway, we'd all rather have people like you living here than some of those horrors who just buy up places like this to use for occasional show-off weekends, or because it's so convenient for Gatwick Airport.'

They had reached the south-facing aspect by this time and were standing in the warm sunshine on the terrace, looking down at the lake below and the gentle slope of the Downs beyond. And in the distance, hidden by the trees, a pair of eyes observed them with amusement and disapproval.

'This really is a superb outlook,' Janet said. 'I do hope they're not planning to ruin it.'

'I shouldn't think so. There's not much building you can do on a lake. Come and have a squint at the inside. This room behind us is the dining room, as far as I remember, but it's quite large enough to be divided into two.'

She had been moving towards the house as she spoke and by then was pressed up against a tall, Georgian-style window, shielding her eyes with both hands and peering inside. A moment later she dropped her hands and spun round, her mouth open and her eyes staring.

'My dear girl, what on earth's the matter?'

'There's something . . . someone there, I think. I can't make it out. Perhaps it was just a trick of the light. See what you think.'

Mystified, but not altogether displeased to discover that the young person's assurance could be so easily shattered, Janet took her place at the window and immediately had to restrain herself from screaming aloud at the sight which confronted her.

A man was seated with his back to the window, the top half of him sprawled across the dining table in a most awkward and unnatural pose. What appeared to be the handle of a knife was sticking out between his shoulder blades.

'Oh, my God,' she wailed. 'Is he dead, do you suppose?'

'Looks like it,' Miranda said, having regained her sang froid.

'What are we going to do?'

'Only one thing we can do, wouldn't you say? No good trying any of the doors, because they're bound to be bolted and barred, so we'll have to break a window and get in that way. Unfortunately neither of us is wearing the right shoes for that job, so we'd better look around for a lump of masonry.' Miranda bent to scan the undergrowth for a likely-looking stone but Janet's eyes were focused on a small blue box high up on the wall of the house.

'But listen, Miranda, don't you see what that could mean?'

'Yes, of course I do. It means one of us would be able to climb inside and make sure he really is dead, for a start.'

'Yes, but don't you realise that if that burglar alarm is switched on, which it's almost certain to be, it will probably ring in the police station and they could be on their way here in a matter of minutes?'

Miranda finally noticed the blue box. 'Let's hope they are. Isn't that what we want?'

'Yes . . . yes, of course, but you don't think it might be more sensible to go back to the pub where I left my car and telephone from there?'

'But that would mean more delay.'

'I realise that, Miranda, but . . . well, the thing is, if we do it your way, we'll have to stop here until they arrive and then, well, they'll want to know who we are and what we're doing here . . . It could be awkward.'

Seeing it in this light, Miranda had to concede that Janet had a point, since it was no part of her original plan that the news of this adventure should get back to her father or to anyone else, for that matter. However, her conscience refused to be stifled until she had made one more attempt to listen to it and she said, 'Yes, I do understand. I expect you're thinking of your husband and that he might not be best pleased to find you'd got yourself mixed up in some local scandal, but it's going to take at least twenty minutes to get back to Redlye, even if we don't get behind a tractor for most of the way and I do think we should at least try and find out whether that man's still alive before we decide.'

'Oh, my dear, I think you can put that idea right out of your mind. He's dead all right. I've seen too much of this kind of thing on my travels to be mistaken about that. One of our Malaysian servants, Kari, was killed in exactly the same way and it is not something you could ever forget.'

As it happened, this was slightly wide of the truth, since she had not herself seen Kari's corpse, only heard about it afterwards from Geoffrey, but she had no desire at all to get any closer to this one and her sole object was to remove herself from the scene as rapidly as possible. She achieved it too, because Miranda, submitting to the voice of experience, gave in and they walked in silence to her car, with Janet setting out at such a brisk pace that she was already inside, with seat belt fastened by the time Miranda caught her up.

The car park of the pub was almost full when they arrived, for which Janet gave another silent word of thanks. An hour earlier, before the pub opened, hers had been the only car there, but now it was safely and unobtrusively tucked away in the middle of a row of its brothers and sisters. Cutting short her farewells as far as her training would allow, she darted over to it and three minutes later drove past the telephone kiosk in time to see her partner in crime emerging.

Miranda had dialled 999 and asked for

Police. On being connected, she told the duty officer that she was speaking from a call box in order to report a murder at Uppfield Court. She paused for a moment, then repeated the last four words and replaced the receiver.

Part of the burden of guilt she had been carrying for the past half hour began to lift as soon as she had concluded this business and before the end of the journey home she even remembered to stop off at the garden centre and pick up a box of petunias. She abandoned for the time being the thought of paying a certain social call, which had been part of her original intention when she had set out on this ill-fated morning.

——Four——

At midday on the following morning Superintendent Wiseman tapped on the door of Billy Jones's studio and walked inside. He was aware of the rules which had been laid down to protect Billy from this kind of invasion, but did not consider himself to be bound by them on this occasion, his call being loosely connected with official business.

'Morning, Bill. Sorry to disturb you during working hours, but something's cropped up which I'd like to have your views on.'

'Well, sit down, then. I can offer you whisky and water, or a glass of sherry,' Billy said, peering into a large corner cupboard, where, as well as assorted gumboots, reference books and typewriter ribbons, he kept a stock of refreshments for favoured visitors.

'Sherry will do nicely, thank you.'

'I assume you're talking about the funny goings-on at Uppfield,' Billy said, pouring a glass for each of them.

'Your assumption is correct.'

'Have you caught him yet?'

'No and not likely to, in my opinion.'

'Really? I should have thought it was a fairly narrow field.'

'Rather too narrow, as it happens. That's the trouble.'

'Well, you asked for my thoughts on the subject and the first one that occurs to me is that the most likely culprit was one of the domestic staff.'

'Mine too, in which case no crime has been committed, according to the book. Even trespass or illegal entry has to be ruled out in their case.'

'None of them resident, are they?'

'No. There used to be a married couple at the Lodge until a few weeks ago. It appears that she did the cooking and he drank the wages. Waddington sent them packing about a week before he went abroad and they won't be replaced until he gets back. Would you mind telling me how you heard about what happened at the weekend?'

'Mrs Wilkes, Ted's wife, told me. She works there five mornings a week and occasional evenings, by arrangement. She has instructions, when Waddington's away, to contact me in cases of emergency and, considering a call she had from your men yesterday afternoon to fall into that category, she rang me up as soon as they had left. She was in a terrible lather because the burglar alarm hadn't gone off. She swears blind that she had switched it on when she left Uppfield on Friday but I expect she just forgot. I suppose everyone thereabouts knew that the Lodge was unoccupied last weekend?'

'Yes, indeed.'

'How about the other domestics? Any of them around?'

'For part of the time, in theory anyway, but it's all pretty haphazard. There are five altogether. Some work one morning a week, others two or three, or a couple of after-noons, in one case. Two of them have their own cars and the rest either get a lift or come on their bikes.'

'Do they all have keys?'

'Not all, no, but I daresay there wasn't much to stop any of them getting hold of a set, if they had a mind to.'

'A mind to stuffing a sack with straw, decking it out in one of Waddington's jack-ets and hats and placing it with its back to the window and a knife sticking out of it?'

'That about covers it, yes. Can you make any sense of it?'

'Not much, no. Presumably, it had been set up for the owner himself to walk in and discover, but one can hardly see that hap-pening, even if someone hadn't seen it first and alerted your men. I realise that the whole staff would have had the day off on Bank Holiday, but obviously the full roster would have been back by this morning and then what? They might or might not have got in touch with you, but are we to believe that they would simply have left the thing spread over the table until Waddington re-turned to enjoy the joke? If so, it must have been a conspiracy between the whole bunch.'

'Not necessarily, old boy.'

'Why not?'

'Because I am prepared to believe that a certain laxity takes over these mice when the cat's away. I daresay they clocked in as usual, but they wouldn't have broken their necks to get there on time or stay until the last whistle blew. There can't be much for them to do at times like these and they're not likely to have invented work for themselves. I daresay the dining room isn't used all that often even when the Master's at home, and a weekly dusting is probably about as much as it would get when he's not. You see what I'm driving at?'

'Oh yes, I think so. You're suggesting that the dining room was chosen deliberately as the scene for this prank, in order that Waddington should be the one to discover it, or at any rate to hear about it the minute someone else did.'

'Precisely.'

'And that it should be recognised as a threat of some kind?'

'That would be the obvious explanation.'

'There is one thing I don't understand, however.'

'No?'

'It sounds to me as though you had

worked out the scenario entirely to your own satisfaction, which is just as it should be, but, since you also maintain that no crime has been committed, why do you go to the trouble of coming here to ask my opinion?'

'Ah!'

'That's not much of an answer. Let me top up your sherry to help you think of a better one.'

'Thank you, I will have a little more. You're not such a fool as you would sometimes have us believe, are you, Bill? And, since you ask, I will tell you the truth. When the telephone message came through my chaps were obliged to treat it seriously, despite the ninety per cent chance of its being some Bank Holiday joker at work, and two cars were despatched. One went up to the Court and the other stopped off at Redlye to make a few enquiries; whether anyone had seen strangers around, unfamiliar cars and so on. You can imagine the kind of thing, but concentrating mainly, of course, on the anonymous lady telephone caller.'

'They concluded Redlye had been her base?'

'Logical enough, seeing that it's got the nearest public telephone box to Uppfield.

It was a forlorn hope, nonetheless, because the village was pretty deserted at that time of the morning, with all the shops closed.'

'So nothing came of it?'

'Oh yes, something did, although by sheer fluke, as it happened. The Constable had about given up and had gone back to his car. However, while he was sitting there, writing up his notes, a tractor came by and he recognised the driver as a young man named Gareth Wilkes, Ted's son. He thought it was worth one more shot and went over to pass the time of day with him and try him out on the same set of questions.'

'*Et voilà!* Eureka!'

'As you say, and my sole excuse for disrupting your morning in this way. Wilkes said he only remembered having seen one car during the past couple of hours and that had been in the lane which leads up from the village to the Lodge gates, until which point it had been behind him the whole way, giving rise to the thought that it was most likely to be making for Uppfield.'

'I should say he was right.'

'So would I. The only curious thing about the incident was that he claimed to have recognised it as your car.'

'In that case, he must have been mistaken.'

'I thought he must be. Just as a matter of interest, though, and to quash any false rumours, would you have any objection to telling me where in fact your car was between ten A.M. and midday yesterday?'

'None whatever. It was sitting in its garage and its owner was hard at work in here.'

'On a Bank Holiday? What a conscientious fellow you are!'

'Nothing conscientious about it, I assure you. For the self-employed Bank Holidays are no different from any other day, except in so far as one is less likely to be interrupted.'

'How about Miranda? She's not self-employed.'

Billy by this time had closed his eyes, as though in deep thought. This was illusory, however, because he had already anticipated the question and worked out the answer.

'No, Miranda didn't take the car out yesterday morning either.'

'How can you be sure of that when you say that you were out here, hard at work?'

'For the simple reason that neither she nor anyone else could have taken the car out because the keys were missing. You may remember our mentioning the fact at Avril's party? We had to get a lift from Martha, which made us all a trifle late.'

'I do remember, now you mention it. Are they still missing?'

'Oh no, all's well again now. They turned up yesterday afternoon in the most obvious place of all, although where exactly that was I either haven't been told, or have forgotten.'

'Well, that's that, then,' Tubby said, setting his glass down and heaving his portly person out of the chair. 'I'd been thinking to myself what a stroke of luck it was your being at Uppfield yesterday morning. Your trained eye might have noticed something which would have given us a clue to the identity of this joker and what his game is. Still, there it is. Things rarely turn out to be as simple as they appear on the surface. I wonder you don't get yourself a spare set of keys,' he added, as Billy accompanied him back to his own car, which was parked in front of the garage.

'We did have one, of course, but that managed to hide itself away in the most obvious place ages ago and I've never bothered to replace it. Having two sets would only make twice as much trouble.'

It flashed into Billy's mind that keys did not inexplicably disappear and reappear when his only child was not in residence and hoped there was nothing more sinister in Miranda's outing yesterday morning than the box of petunias, dumped outside the garage door, awaiting transportation to their London window box, seemed to imply.

——Five——————————

1

The news of the macabre practical joke had by this time spread to every household in the neighbourhood, causing great hilarity among the anti-development league and tears of relief to be shed in private by Janet Gillford.

'Where on earth did you hear all this?' Geoffrey asked when she told him about it at lunch. 'There was no mention of it in any of the papers this morning. Not that I've had time to do more than skim them,' he added, recollecting himself.

'No, it was Avril who told me, when I rang her up to thank her for Sunday. She seemed to think it was a great joke. She also told me that Robert was back. He'd just stepped inside the house, but she didn't have the fun of breaking the news to him because he'd heard it already.'

'Really? I was given to understand that he'd been in the States for the past four or five days.'

'So he had, but he travelled back on the same plane as Mr Waddington and some lady friend of his. Wasn't that an extraordinary coincidence? Apparently, the police had been in touch with him by telephone and he decided to come back immediately and help them sort things out, although they assured him it wouldn't be necessary.'

'And that, I would say, would be exactly the kind of situation to appeal to your friend, Avril.'

'Why would you say so?'

'I could be wrong, but I like to think I can recognise her type of woman from a mile off.'

'What type of woman are you talking about, Geoffrey?'

'One who likes to assert herself and interfere in matters which are no concern of hers. Rather too bossy and aggressive for my taste, I'm afraid, if you don't mind my saying so.'

Janet did not in the least mind his saying so and would have encouraged him to indulge in further censures and criticisms of her dear friend, if it made him happy. However, there was one small hurdle which needed to be cleared before the subject of Mr Waddington was allowed to drop and she had decided to face it head on.

'It's such a strange coincidence, you know, Geoffrey, but I found myself very near Uppfield yesterday. Now I think of it, I realise that it could have been swarming with policemen by that time, so perhaps it's just as well I didn't get any nearer.'

'What? What are you on about, Janet? What time was this?'

'Oh, elevenish, I suppose. Can't have been any later because I was back here by twelve.'

'But what on earth induced you to go there at all?'

'Well, I had nothing special to do, you see. No shopping, of course, so I thought I might as well potter off and have a look at that house at Maresfield they'd sent us particulars of.'

'Why didn't you get Anthony to go with you?'

'Because Anthony hates looking at houses

and, anyway, he wasn't even dressed by the time I was ready to leave.'

Janet, by this time, was growing rather resentful of being forced into telling so many untruths, but she ploughed gamely on: 'Anyway, the Maresfield house was a complete dud, nothing like the photograph. It was much too small for us and with a perfectly hideous villa practically cheek by jowl. So there I was, sitting in the car and feeling rather flat and when I looked at the road map I saw that Uppfield was only four or five miles away, so, having come all that way, I thought I might as well have something to show for it and the next thing was that I had the most extraordinary stroke of luck.'

'Indeed? What was that?'

'I came to a village called Redlye, which we'd been through on our way to Avril's, when I saw that Jones girl getting into her car. You remember her? Miranda, she's called. So I went over and asked for directions to Uppfield. She said it was only a mile or two, but rather complicated if you hadn't been there before and she very kindly offered to drive me up there herself. Wasn't it sweet of her?'

'Oh, very. What was she doing in Red-lye?'

'How should I know? Presumably it's their local village, but it was none of my business and it didn't occur to me to ask. The offer was going and, having got that far, I decided to take it.'

'But you say you didn't go right up to the house?'

'No, it wasn't necessary. The drive straightens out about half way there and you can see it spread out before you, in all its horror.'

'How do you mean, horror?'

'Simply that it's the most hideous and gloomy old mausoleum you could ever imagine. Mr Jones must have had a very odd impression of us if he seriously imagined we could contemplate living in such a place. Apart from all the other disadvantages, it's much too isolated. Two miles, at least, from the nearest shop or post office and I don't suppose very much gets delivered up there. It wouldn't matter for young people, I daresay, but at our time of life we have to plan ahead for our old age.'

Geoffrey's expression indicated that he had no desire whatever to do any such thing and, to cover her *faux pas,* she said, 'Anyway, you were right, as usual. It was an insane idea.'

'I can't think why you expected anything else, or bothered to go there, in the first place.'

'Oh, just curiosity, I suppose. And then finding myself so near and with everything made so easy for me, I couldn't resist it. Besides . . .'

'Besides what?'

'Well, you know, Geoffrey, I still can't help wondering about this Mr Waddington. It's not such a very common name, after all. I realise he can't be the brother of the one you knew in Singapore, because we're told he was the only son, but he could be a cousin or something and . . . well, despite what you said, I mean I'm sure you'll tell me I'm wrong, but I do seem to remember he had a scar on his forehead just like the one they described.'

'If that's what you believe, my dear, then it must be true. Who am I to argue? And, besides, what difference does it make? Even if whoever told me about his being killed in a car crash had confused him with someone else, how would it concern us? I haven't set eyes on the man for nearly ten years and, for all I care, he could just as well be dead.

As for the here and now, there's only one thing that matters and let us be thankful for it.'

'Oh? What's that?'

'That, in view of what's happened there, not a living soul knows that you went to look at Uppfield Court on Monday morning.'

'Except Miranda Jones, of course.'

'Ah, yes, that's a nuisance. I'd forgotten about her. Still, at least it means, if there should be any talk about it, she'll be able to confirm that you didn't go near the house.'

2

Miranda and Billy were also having lunch which, so far and much to his relief, had passed without bickering or acrimony, Miranda having scarcely uttered a word since they sat down.

He attributed this to the fact that she had spent most of the morning upstairs in the old nursery, which he had re-designed and fitted out as a practice studio, complete with barre and elaborate musical equipment. This had been one of the few jobs around the house which he had undertaken with enthusiasm and had afterwards seen as time and money well spent and a great asset in his campaign to ward off her attempts to tidy up the studio whenever she felt bored or restless. However, he occasionally re-membered that he had other parental duties as well and he said, 'You seem to be off your food and you are looking a trifle pale and wan. Perhaps you have been rather over-doing the exercises this morning?'

'On the contrary, I have spent most of it sitting on the floor, listening to Chopin.'

'Oh, dear. You are not ill, I hope?'

'No, worse than that. I feel I am heading towards a Montague/Capulet situation and I need your co-operation to straighten it out.'

'You wish me to sketch out a few designs for a balcony?'

'Really, Pa, I do wish you wouldn't joke about absolutely everything.'

'No joke, I assure you. It was probably one of the most selfless offers you have ever received from me. As you are all too well aware, I have a great deal of pressing work on hand at present.'

'Yes, I am and that is the crux of the matter. I should like it better if you could forget this pressing work of yours and switch your mind and talents to something less offensive to the neighbours.'

'I know you would. We have been through this argument twice already and I have endeavoured to explain to you that my retiring from the fray would have no effect at all on the eventual outcome. I have no power to prevent the organisers going ahead with this scheme, so long as there's a chance of their making a few billions out of it, and if I were to drop out they would simply find someone to replace me. By working with, instead of against them, I may at least be able to exert some influence over the way they go about it and, with a bit of luck, perhaps ensure that whatever they do is done with a modicum of taste and style. I haven't bothered to explain all this to anyone else.'

'Because you're too proud and hoity-toity?'

'No, because if they haven't seen it for themselves, my pointing it out will do nothing to convince them. And what do I care? You, of course, are different.'

'In what way am I different?'

'First of all, you're my daughter and since, in the nature of things, we are likely to be stuck with each other for a good many years, it would be preferable for us to remain on good terms. Secondly, you only come down here at irregular intervals and therefore cannot be expected to be *au courant* with new developments and, thirdly, unlike the vast majority of my critics, you have no incentive to safeguard your own interests against all comers.'

'What does all that mean?'

'Simply that practically all the most vociferous objectors to this scheme, however much they may rant and rave and write letters to *The Times* about the conservation of the landscape and the iniquity of despoiling our national heritage for a mess of potage, are really only concerned with the decline in value it will bring to their own properties.'

'I'm not sure I agree with you there,' Miranda said, refilling her glass with mineral water and slicing an apple into neat symmetrical quarters. 'Take Martha, for instance. I can't see her being bothered by such a thing.'

'I did say practically all.'

'Okay, so here's something else you've left out of your calculations. You're wrong in thinking that I have no incentive to safeguard my own interests, because that's just what I bloody well have to do.'

'Because there will be less for you to inherit when I die? Is that what you mean?'

'You know damn well it isn't. This is a different brand of self-interest. You may have heard me mention earlier that I am the innocent victim of a bitter family feud?'

'Oh, so we're back with the Montagus and Capulets again, are we? That's good. I'd been meaning to ask you where they belong in our lives.'

'Nowhere yet, but I am seriously considering the idea of marrying young Mr Montagu and Montagu senior is one of those who strongly disapprove of your current client. It would suit me better if you would have nothing further to do with him.'

'I daresay it would, but I shall need a little more persuading before I commit myself to that extent. When did the idea of marrying this young man flit into your head?'

'At about two o'clock yesterday afternoon when he proposed to me.'

'I see. And how long have you known him?'

'Oh, for at least two months.'

'Really, Miranda, it is asking rather a lot to expect me to sacrifice my career, not to mention let myself in for damages, for the sake of such a short acquaintance. Have I met these people?'

'I shouldn't think so, but they seem to know all about you and when young Mr Montagu heard what my surname was he said that if he and I were to have an ongoing relationship it might be advisable to change it by deed poll.'

'But you decided that it would be simpler to do so by marrying him.'

'No, that came later.'

'But you did manage to find out what his surname was?'

'Yes, naturally. I could hardly commit myself to such a serious step without doing so. It is Rupert Crossman. That's not too bad, do you think? Miranda Crossman sounds quite distinguished.'

'Ah, Rupert Crossman, son of James, who owns the house the Gillfords are now living in, so I hope for their sake that you are not planning an early wedding. On the other hand, it sounds to me as though the thing is likely to fizzle out long before you get to that stage.'

'Why does it sound to you like that?'

'Because he seems to make a practice of this sort of thing. According to Mrs Gill-

74

ford, he has only just broken off his engagement to some other female.'

'Yes, I know. He told me all about that and he realises now that what he felt for her wasn't love at all. She was just the Rosaline of the play, which makes it all the more poignant. Romeo had dallied with her a bit, but as soon as he clapped eyes on Juliet she meant nothing to him at all.'

'Well, that's all right then, and now that I know who his father is, I see no reason for him to make all this fuss about the development scheme. It's several miles from where he lives and won't impinge on him at all.'

'It's not as simple as you think. He loathes and despises Mr Waddington for all sorts of other reasons, quite apart from what he's up to now, and the dislike covers everyone who's in league with him or working on his side.'

'What other reasons?'

'Well, to give you an example, he's supposed to have done a more or less criminal thing to Rupert's father, who at the time Mr Waddington first took over the estate owned some land adjoining Uppfield. Despite the fact that Mr Waddington and the Crossmans were on very good terms at the time, playing golf together and going to each other's houses for dinner and that sort of thing, Waddington's greed got the better of him and apparently, he tricked Mr Crossman out of an acre and a half of this land, which he said belonged by rights to him and he'd found some old deeds or something to prove it. Naturally, Mr Crossman didn't give in and hand it over without a struggle, but Mr Waddington hired the most expensive QC he could find and won the case. So then what do you think?'

'I've no idea.'

'Mr Waddington had claimed that he needed that bit of land to put up a cottage for one of his cowmen and he built the most hideous and grotesque villa you could possibly imagine and after a few months, lo and behold, the cowman left, the villa was empty and he sold it to some ghastly weekenders at a vast profit, needless to say, who promptly added on a foul-looking conservatory, plus garage, and all their friends come romping down from London, churning up the lanes with their huge and horrible cars. And to top it all, while the two men were fighting it out in the courts, Mrs Crossman suddenly got ill and died and Rupert's father blames her death on the worry about this Waddington business. So you can see you're not very popular in that quarter.'

'None of this had anything to do with me, you know, and it does nothing to alter my attitude to Waddington's current shenanigans. However, I promise to give careful consideration to everything you've told me before coming to a final decision. How will that do?'

'Okay,' Miranda said, getting to work on her second apple. 'I'm quite willing to go along with that, especially as I consider you're bound to change your mind and live to be glad of it.'

'Do you, indeed? Then before you get too complacent, just hear me out for two minutes. All of us around here, including me, occasionally remember to give thanks for being able to wake up every morning to the sight of hedgerows and meadows and sheep grazing on the Downs, but we rarely do so with wonder and amazement. We have come to believe that it is our divine right that not so much as a blade of grass should ever be changed.'

'And so it was until those predators came along and tried to grab it and turn it into money.'

'That's true, in a sense. Very few people

apply themselves to any project unless there is some reward to be gained from it, but that's not the whole story, you know. The countryside, as we know it now, was not always like this. It has no resemblance to Nature in the raw. Changes were made to cultivate and tame it, largely for the benefit of the landowners, I might add, and these darling hedges and copses were planted there for a purpose. Changes will continue to be made and one might as well accept the fact. Better in the end to swim with the tide than against it and make the best of what you have left is my motto.'

'I know that and you make it sound very wise and noble, but I call it defeatist. There are much more constructive things you could be doing.'

'Such as?'

'Well, for instance, I've heard of masses of people who are getting up petitions and protest marches and slaving away to raise money for lawyers to get the planning application turned down.'

'Yes, I know and jolly good luck to them, if that's the way they feel but, if they do succeed, the scheme will only be shelved until the opposing forces have re-grouped and are ready to bring it out again in so-called modified form. The most they can hope for is that a new site will be chosen twenty or even thirty miles away and, with any luck, it will become someone else's problem. The sad truth is that this is one of the most affluent parts of the country, which is one reason for it having been artificially preserved for so long. But it also means that there is virtually no unemployment. Less favoured citizens of the realm have now realised this and are clamouring to take advantage of it. You can hardly blame them, but it does mean that for every individual here who wants to keep things exactly as they are, there are twenty families urgently needing somewhere to live in a place where there is some employment. It all depends on which side of the fence you come from. However, we've agreed to call a truce, so let's leave it there for the time being.'

These well considered sentiments hid a vast amount of unease on Billy Jones's part. For although the tale of the litigation over the land adjoining Uppfield was entirely new to him, he did recall some gossip concerning the death of the late Mrs Crossman which at the time he dismissed as idle tittle-tattle, but which, in view of recent developments, he would have to reassess. All in all, he rather wished that Miranda's eyes had fallen upon a suitor far removed from the county of Sussex.

3

At the same time as Billy Jones was being plagued by uneasy thoughts and Miranda went on eating her apple unconcernedly, Martha picked up the telephone and dialled one of the few numbers she had no need to check in her address book.

'Would you be at home if I were to look in some time this afternoon, Avril?'

'As far as I know. What's on your mind?'

'It's a bit tricky. I can't very well explain on the telephone.'

'How exciting! Come about four or four-thirty and we'll discuss it over the teacups.'

'Are you sure I won't be interrupting anything?'

'Quite sure,' Avril replied, interpreting the question correctly. 'Robert's in London for the day and he won't be back till after seven.'

'Thank you. I just need some advice, you see.'

'And I'm always ready with that, as you know. See you later.'

'You know Mrs Bailey, who comes to me two mornings a week?' Martha was saying about two hours later.

'Of course, I do, known her all my life. She was a Wilkes, wasn't she?'

'Not quite, but her sister is married to one, so it comes to the same thing. I should explain that Tuesday is not her regular day, but, as yesterday was a Bank Holiday and her husband was at home, she came this morning instead.'

Avril could have been forgiven for asking why it was necessary to explain any such thing, but, aware of Martha's inability to approach any subject other than through a tangle of excuses and apologies, she only nodded.

'She was a bit early too, as it happens, and I rather suspected she'd just come to say she couldn't come, if you see what I mean, although if I'd been thinking straight, I'd have realised that, in that case, she'd have rung me up and in fact she was in such a hurry to tell me her troubles that she could hardly wait to get her coat off.'

'Admirable woman,' Avril said. 'No wonder you prize her. What were they?'

'Something her sister, Alice, the one who's married to Ted Wilkes, had been round to her house to ask her advice about yesterday evening. Well, to come straight to the point, I suppose you've heard about that funny business at Uppfield and how they found a dummy figure, with a knife sticking out of it?'

'Certainly, I have. The entire neighbourhood is buzzing with the story and one or two people have a shrewd suspicion that a member of the Wilkes clan was responsible. I suppose you've come to tell me they're right?'

'My dear Avril, of course not. What can you be thinking of?'

'Well, I admit that it would surprise me if they should own up. So, if not that, what is the problem?'

'Just what you started by saying. A lot of people have got the idea that one of them did it because of course they all know that Ted and his family are threatened with being turned out, to make way for a golf course, or whatever, not to mention the fact that his wife has keys to the house and can walk in whenever she pleases.'

'Yes, pretty black all round, you might say.'

'And worse to come, I'm afraid.'

'Go on, then. Tell me the lot.'

'It concerns the jacket that object was dressed in. According to Mrs Bailey, Alice didn't see it because it had been removed by the police by the time anyone was allowed into the house, but the worry is that she did take one of Mr Waddington's jackets home with her a few weeks ago.

'You don't say? Whatever for?'

'He'd torn a sleeve on a branch or bit of barbed wire, or something. She noticed it when she was tidying up one morning and she thought she might as well take it home and mend it for him.'

'And then forgot to put it back again?'

'No, no, you keep getting so near the truth and then giving it a twist at the end. Two days later she took it back and hung it up in the gun room, where it lived.'

'So why the panic?'

'Because she's the only one who knows she put it back and, if it should turn out to be the same one, that's to say one with a newly-darned sleeve, that the dummy was wearing, she's going to have a hard time getting anyone to believe her.'

'Yes, very annoying. Isn't it sad how often acts of kindness rebound on us? On the other hand, she may well be lying through her teeth and, if she didn't rig up this pranky corpse herself, has a strong suspicion that one of her relatives probably did.'

'I don't agree, Avril, I honestly don't. I mean, if you're right, why would she be blurting it out to all and sundry? She must have known Mrs Bailey would pass it on to me. In fact, I have the impression that she was intended to.'

'You bet she was. No fool, that Alice, and cunning with it, like all the Wilkes family.'

'But what's cunning about producing all the evidence against herself, if she really was the culprit? More sensible, I should have thought, to lie low and hope no one would ever discover she had taken the jacket home.'

'Don't be dotty, Martha. Waddington will remember, even if all the rest of the staff weren't in the know. And, if she's innocent, why does she assume so easily that this jacket was the one that was used?'

'Which it may not have been, for all we know.'

'I'm willing to bet it was, though, and that when the time came to put it back it had been removed and she has a damn good idea by whom.'

'So what ought Mrs Bailey advise her to do now?'

'Nothing, as far as I can see. If she sticks to her story that the last time she saw the jacket was when she put it back in the gun room, it's going to be difficult to prove she's lying. And, since the only crime to have been committed is likely to be wilful damage to an article of clothing, I doubt if anyone's going to bother very much, apart from the local gossipmongers. Naturally, everyone will take it for granted that the Wilkes family were behind this somewhat malicious jape, but not many will think the worse of them for that and, in a few days or weeks, a new sensation will come along and this one will be forgotten. And, talking of that, do you want to hear my news?'

'Yes, indeed I do, especially if it's likely to create a new sensation.'

'I'm hoping it will. You know, of course, that Eric Walker, our own dear, ineffectual Rural District Councillor, dropped off his perch last week?'

'I did hear, yes. You're not going to tell me there was something fishy about it?'

'No, certainly not. He had a heart attack while watching television, which is something that could happen to any of us. However, that's not the end of the story because what it means is that in roughly three weeks from today we shall all be trotting down to the village hall to cast our votes for his replacement.'

'Yes, I suppose we shall. I wonder who we'll get this time?'

'Interesting, isn't it? Especially with this development scheme hanging over us. Who would you choose?'

'Oh, how would I know? I'm completely ignorant about politics.'

'Politics have nothing to do with it, or, at any rate, shouldn't have. What it needs is someone with an intimate knowledge of the four or five parishes concerned and the needs and wishes of those who live in them, and who is not afraid to speak up on their behalf.'

'My dear Avril, you begin to sound as though you're making an electioneering speech yourself. Oh, now don't tell me! I've fallen right into it, haven't I? You've been invited to stand as the new candidate?'

'Not exactly, no. Not the official party one, that is. They did suggest I should have a go, as it happens, but I said that, although deeply honoured and grateful, I felt obliged to decline. How am I doing? Getting the jargon off rather pat, don't you think?'

'Very pat indeed, but isn't it rather a waste of effort, since you felt obliged to decline?'

'Ah, but there's more to come. The reason for feeling obliged to decline was because, as I've told you, I didn't fancy the idea of toeing the party line simply because they've adopted me as their candidate. There could well be a conflict of interests there, and I should be in bad odour if I voted against them. Whereas just opting out and abstaining wouldn't be any use to anyone. All the same, it was a bit disappointing having to turn it down. I rather saw myself as Councillor Meyer, turning up late for parties and explaining that I'd just come from a meeting at the Town Hall. And then up pops Robert, who is always so clever at finding a way round things, with the perfect solution.'

'Does he think you should join the Opposition?'

'Oh, dear me, no, that would be just as

bad, if not worse. Robert's idea is that I should go it alone and stand as an Independent.'

'Oh, my dear Avril, what a splendid idea! In that way you'll be able to tell both sides off.'

'Quite so, and he's going to act as my agent and absolutely swamp the neighbourhood with pamphlets full of high-sounding slogans. He's even arranged for a photographer to come down from London and take some pictures of me looking keen and forthright; and when there's something important on I shall be able to rely on him to write a really inspiring speech for me. That's if I get in, of course.'

'Oh, you're bound to. You've got masses of friends round here.'

'Well, do your best to keep them up to the mark, will you? I shall expect them all, including Baileys and Wilkes, to rally to the flag on polling day.'

'Although not including Billy Jones, I take it?'

'Well, you know, I'm not so sure of that, Martha. This is no time to be defeatist and I have hopes of him yet.'

──Six────────────────────────

1

On Sunday morning, a week after Avril's luncheon party, Geoffrey announced that he would be going up to London the following day and would spend the night at his club.

This had happened once or twice during the few weeks they had spent at Dormer Hill and, in the normal way, Janet would have displayed only a token interest, three-quarters of her mind having already swept ahead to dwell on the pleasant prospect of a good turn-out of the library.

However, Geoffrey had been unusually distrait the previous evening, hardly rousing himself to criticise or complain about anything, and also there was something self-conscious in the heavily casual way in which he broke the news and she said, 'Oh, that's nice. It will make a little break for you. Why don't you drive up with Anthony this evening?'

'For a number of reasons,' he replied, reverting to a more characteristic style. 'In the first place, I do not at all relish being driven for fifty miles in that noisy little perambulator he calls a car. Secondly, my first appointment tomorrow is at twelve-thirty and I have no desire to spend longer in London than I have to. Thirdly, I could hardly justify the expense of two nights at the club when one would be enough. I am not made of money, you know.'

It was an assertion he often made and, if Janet had still been under the illusion that he was made of money, she would certainly not have deserved her reputation for being a good listener.

'I realise that,' she said, 'but at least you wouldn't have to pay the train fare and taxi from the station, so you would save that much.'

'A point which Anthony would be unlikely to overlook and would inevitably expect me to shell out for the petrol, so I don't see myself gaining much there. Do I dream it, or are you rather eager to be rid of me?'

'Don't be silly, Geoffrey, you know perfectly well I'm not. It's just that I thought it might make a change for you to get out of the rut and spend a little time in London, for once. It's not so important for me. I can always find plenty to do in the house and garden, but you must feel awfully hemmed in sometimes, after the sort of life you're used to.'

'Naturally, I wouldn't have the temerity to compare my work with yours, but it is quite demanding enough to keep me fully occupied, I assure you. In fact, my first appointment tomorrow happens to be with an acquaintance of mine who is quite a big shot in the world of publishing. If I get the kind of reaction from him I'm hoping for, I fancy I shall have even less time to spare for trips to London.'

'Oh well, that is good news. Congratulations! What a dark horse you are, though, Geoffrey, leaving it to the last minute to tell me that bit. I do hope it all works out well for you.'

'Thank you, my dear. You shall be the first to know if it does. Oh, and by the way,' he added, making a neat job of folding the newspaper, which he had recently formed the habit of taking into the library with him before she had read it. 'Please, on no account, attempt to re-arrange anything on my desk while I'm away. I realise what a muddle it must look to someone as tidy and well-organised as yourself, but I like to jot down ideas as they occur to me and it would be such a help to come back and find every-thing just as I left it.'

'Why, Geoffrey, you must know me bet-ter than that. It would never occur to me to lay so much as a finger on your papers.'

He acknowledged the truth of this and she continued to smile after he had left the room. She was thinking how pleasant it was to be married to a man who, for all his funny little weaknesses, was so high principled himself as to be incapable of suspecting those about him of being capable of deceit or double-dealing.

2

Miranda was also making plans for depar-ture by the fast train on Monday morning, although, lacking the benefit of thirty years' training, hers were not conducted on quite the same harmonious level as Janet had managed to achieve.

'What time should we leave for the sta-tion?' Billy asked on Sunday evening.

'Not later than eight-twenty. Give me a shout if I'm not down by half past seven, will you? I'm liable to fall asleep after the alarm goes and I have one or two things to see to before I leave.'

'At least you won't have to bother much about packing, since you intend to return on Friday.'

'Very true. If that's okay with you?'

'You know very well it is. This is your home, after all. At any rate, for the time being.'

'And you promise to give some thought between now and Friday to what we were talking about last night?'

'Yes, I have already promised, but please don't go away with any illusions that your battle is already won because I feel bound to say that, having given some thought to it already, I have a feeling that your argument is going to make very little difference to my decision.'

'Oh, thanks very much. After all that fine talk about my happiness mattering most.'

'And so it does, but the trouble is, Miranda, that so far I have failed to convince myself that sacrificing my beliefs in order for you to ingratiate yourself with your prospective father-in-law is really going to lead to the ultimate happiness of either of us. Who knows where that sort of thing might end? If he were to get his way over this, he might take a whim for me to take up jogging or become a Mason.'

'Oh, don't be ridiculous. You know perfectly well that's complete twaddle and also that it's not just a whim. He can't bear the idea of his son being involved with someone whose father is the crony and partner of his hated enemy.'

'Which is what I call a whim; the whim of a self-important arrogant nit-wit. Whoever heard of such nonsense in this day and age? I am sorry if I offend you.'

'No need to apologise because I rather agree with you, as it happens. The fact remains though that he's got it firmly stuck in his stubborn head that your friend Waddington was morally responsible for his wife's untimely death and is about to increase his already not inconsiderable wealth partly with land gained from the Crossman family by legal trickery and, whether you consider that far-fetched or not, the truth is that it is a disgusting way to behave. The fact that you are aiding and abetting him is the last straw and makes you public enemy Number Two.'

'Nevertheless, if this young man of yours—what did you say his name was?'

'Rupert.'

'If Rupert has any spunk at all he's hardly likely to cast you off like a spent match simply because your parents don't see eye to eye.'

'No, of course not, but you must see that it won't exactly create a harmonious atmosphere.'

'Oh, why worry about that? You'll have more important things to think about.'

'Yes, like the wedding, for instance. Naturally, we'd hoped to have it down here, with all our friends, but what's the use of trying to plan anything like that if half the congregation isn't speaking to the other half and Rupert's father refuses to sign any document which has your name on it?'

'Oh, I see. So now I am required to sacrifice myself on the altar of social convention? Things have come to a pretty pass and, in any case, I consider you are taking too much for granted. You only met the young man a few weeks ago and I consider all this talk about weddings to be unbecomingly hasty. I know the young man has seen fit to propose to you on such brief acquaintance but it may be more appropriate to a modern young lady like yourself, with career prospects and all that, to consider the matter well before accepting.'

'You really are talking like a Victorian novel, Pa. I always make up my mind about people right from the start and so does Rupert. We both know we are made for each other and we want to get married.'

'Then you had better combine forces and get to work on his father. If you go at it in your usual relentless fashion I am sure you will soon have him eating out of your hand.'

'I shall try that, of course, but you know what I think would be even better, Pa?'

'No. What?'

'If someone would come along and stick a knife into Mr Waddington, making sure to get the man and not a dummy this time, then we could all forget about this rotten scheme of his and go back to being normal and civilised again.'

'Oh, as to that, I entirely agree with you,' Billy said. 'I have thought so all along, though I would, on the whole, advise against making such bloodthirsty statements in public. You never know who might be listening.'

——Seven————————

1

Had it not been for the jauntily casual way in which he asked her not to do so, it might never have occurred to Janet to give more than a cursory glance at Geoffrey's papers, far less to waste precious time reading them. He received very few letters through the post, fewer still of a personal nature and those that did arrive from old friends or relatives were invariably passed over to her to read for herself and often to be answered by herself, as well.

Nor had she felt any particular curiosity about his manuscript, since she privately believed that he was unlikely ever to finish it and that, if she were mistaken about this, she would inevitably be required to type it out for him, not once but several times. In any case, the precious notebooks containing the memoirs were absent, no doubt carried off to London to be perused by the big shot in the world of publishing.

On this occasion, however, having made a thorough job of sweeping and dusting, polishing the fire irons and washing the paintwork, she indulged herself by fetching a steaming mug of coffee from the kitchen and buckling down to an inspection of the contents of his desk. Ten minutes later she was still sitting there, feeling that her whole life had been blown to pieces and scattered to the winds.

It had been a job which could not be hurried because she had first to imprint an impression on her mind as to how everything had looked at the outset, so that not so much as an envelope or pencil in the wrong place should give her away and several rehearsals were needed before she could retain a true picture with her eyes shut.

In contrast, the search itself had taken no more than three or four minutes, at the end of which her sly little trick had rebounded on herself to the point where not only had her legs gone into open rebellion against such messages as her brain might send them to support her weight when she stood up, but she could see little point in trying to argue them out of it.

Strangely enough, although physically shattered by the shock, she also felt mentally stimulated, exactly as though she had had too much to drink and her inhibitions were melting away. Indeed, her first thought, before her legs imposed their ban, had been to pour herself a large brandy and it was not until she remembered that Geoffrey, unable or unwilling to break the habits he had formed when they had half a dozen servants, would have locked the drinks cabinet and taken the key to London with him.

The letter which had brought all this disturbance into her well-ordered life had been tucked away inside a shiny brochure, informing Geoffrey that among other delights he was one of the chosen few who were eligible to win a brand new car and a holiday for two in the Caribbean and she assumed that this accounted for his unease. He had thrust it in there for whatever reason and had subsequently been unable to find it again or to convince himself that it was not still somewhere among his papers.

However, in her impatience to read the contents, she did not linger over these speculations, nor open the small sheet of folded lined paper which the brochure had also yielded up. The letter itself consisted of two pages of royal blue paper, covered in a rounded childish script which was teasingly familiar. It bore neither address nor date and read as follows:

Darling Geoff, What a sweet thought!!! You are an old pet to send me those gorgeous pink roses. I was quite over-come. In fact (don't laugh) I actually had a little weep when I read the card and saw who they were from. Remember how you always used to bring me pink roses on my birthday? Well, I know I'm not really supposed to write to you at home (and I expect ringing up would be an even worse crime!) but I simply couldn't bear to let another day go by without thanking you for your lovely thought. Anyway, roll on Monday week!!!

It was signed 'Jennifer' and therein lay the sense of betrayal. Janet had always preened herself on seeing a degree of marital infidelity as inevitable, even on occasions acceptable, so long as it was conducted with discretion, asking only that the other women in Geoffrey's life should be transitory and anonymous. An affair with his first wife broke all these rules and added humiliation, as well as insult to her injury.

It was also very unsettling, particularly in this difficult period, with no roof to call their own and she was concentrating so fiercely on trying to adjust to it and to plan her future course of action that she only gave an absent-minded glance at the scrawled incomprehensible note which had fallen out of the brochure, along with Jennifer's letter and a message, written in pencil in Geoffrey's hand, stating merely: 'Mon. 12 Sackville C. S. W.'

Later on it occurred to her that it no doubt signified that Jennifer was now living at 12, Sackville Court, Close, or Crescent, somewhere in South-West London and that Geoffrey at this very moment, and no doubt armed with another bunch of roses, was on his way to see her.

2

Later the same morning, while Janet was composing a letter to an old friend whose husband had just dropped dead, Mr Crossman senior added his mite to the unpleasantness of the day by dropping in for what he called a bit of a chat. This was not an apt description, for he was a burly, red-faced, inarticulate man, punctuating his conversation with long silences and lacking only breeches and a tweed hat to complete the Farmer Giles image, thereby reviving the question of whether people chose the way of life which best fitted their appearance, or the other way round. In Mr Crossman's case, it was probably a little of both, since his father and grandfather had been successful farmers before him.

It was really Geoffrey he had called to see, but when Janet explained that this would not be possible he looked so disconsolate that she relented and said, 'Well, do sit down for a minute, now you're here. I'm afraid I can't offer you a real drink. Anthony had some young friends here at the weekend and they seem to have cleaned us out, but there's still some beer in the refrigerator, if you can manage with that?'

Mr Crossman said that he was not fussy and that beer would be all right and, on her return from the kitchen a few minutes later, he was seated in an armchair, with his knees apart, his hands dangling between them and staring into space.

'Would you mind helping yourself?' she asked. 'I'm so clumsy about opening these tins. Was it something urgent you wanted to talk to Geoffrey about? If so, I'll make sure that he rings you as soon as he gets back tomorrow.'

'No need for that. Happened to be passing, so thought I might as well drop in and get one or two little matters sorted out, but it can wait.'

'I see, and I must say I'm relieved.'

'Why's that, if you don't mind me asking?'

'I'd had a nasty feeling that you'd come to warn us that our days here were numbered.'

'No, nothing like that. Other way round, in fact. I had it in my mind to ask whether he'd consider extending our present arrangement for another six months. That'd bring us up to the end of the year, but of course I wouldn't hold you to it, if you'd found anything permanent and ready to move into by then.'

'That's extremely generous of you, Mr Crossman. I am sure Geoffrey will be delighted to accept your offer, but it does seem a little one-sided.'

'Not to me. As I see it, you're good tenants, but I can't expect you to carry on indefinitely without some security of tenure and what I don't want is to have the house empty and back on my hands at a few weeks' notice. We'd have the vandals and squatters moving in before you could turn round.'

'Yes, but how about your son? I thought he was the one who was keeping us all in suspense?'

'The situation has changed a bit there. I'm beginning to wonder whether he'll want to make his home here now.'

'Oh, don't say that, Mr Crossman. I mean, I realise what a bitter blow it must have been, his fiancée running off with someone else and I can understand that just now he feels he'll never fall in love again for as long as he lives, but we both know it isn't true. In six months, or even less, he'll meet someone new and he'll wonder how he could ever have looked at another girl.'

'I'd like to believe you. Nothing I'd like more than to see him married and settled down in a home of his own, but I doubt if it's a good idea for him to settle in these parts.'

'Oh, but why? This is such a nice house; just the right size and so conveniently situated. So near his work and all his friends, I should have thought it was ideal.'

Mr Crossman shook his head, as though a fly was buzzing round it. 'That's where you make your mistake,' he said, then snapped his lips together with great finality.

Diverted from her own problems, Janet

scented gossip, and prodded the reluctant farmer for more information. 'Well, I don't mean to pry into your private affairs, but are you suggesting that he wants to get right away and start on his own somewhere?'

James Crossman was in a quandary. He genuinely despised talking about his family and since his poor wife died he largely kept himself to himself, discouraging neighbours from making friendly advances. The only bond he felt was with his son and now that too was threatened. Janet Gillford looked so kind and sensible he almost felt that he could trust her.

'I hadn't intended to burden you with all the ins and outs of it. Still, now I've got started, I may as well tell you the lot. No need to pass it on, mind.'

'I shouldn't dream of doing so. I won't even tell Geoffrey, if you'd rather I didn't.'

'That's up to you and it's all going to come out sooner or later, I daresay. You know, of course, that Rupert's girl left him flat, but did you hear what her reason was?'

'I heard rumours. The story is that your son's fiancée had thrown him over for someone terribly rich.'

Rumours! Bitterness overwhelmed the farmer. 'I'll fill in a few of the gaps with facts. He's middle-aged, a good twenty years older than her and he lives in very grand style not so very far from here. You are too new in the district to have come across him but now he's getting this new wife, they're bound to be taking part in all the local do's and giving big parties and all the rest of it and, for my part, I don't see my Rupert taking that in his stride very easily. Imagine the humiliation! I think he's going to want to get as far away as he can, for a few years anyway, and who can blame him?'

Janet's recent discovery made her more sympathetic than usual. A very private infidelity on the part of one's husband could have its uses in reinforcing one's bargaining position on the marital battlefield, but to be practically abandoned at the altar in favour of a wealthy old man was a public humiliation not easily shrugged off. Adept at reading between the lines and also, through her ill-fated Easter Monday jaunt to Uppfield, knowing slightly more than she had allowed the red-faced farmer to believe, though unfortunately not sufficient to prevent her from jumping to the wrong conclusion, Janet would now have been prepared to point an accusing finger at the perpetrator of the straw-stuffed dummy with the knife between the shoulder blades joke. It was fortunate that she was not required to do so, because she would have been shamefully mistaken.

——Eight——

1

Avril Meyer had lost no time in getting her election campaign off the ground. With ten days still to go, voters had been swamped with leaflets, mostly delivered by the Meals-on-Wheels volunteers, as a sideline. Judy Chambers, née Wilkes, who, before her marriage, had been a full-time secretary, came to the house three mornings a week to do the clerical work and another band of willing workers, including Martha, stood by at the ready to drive the old and infirm to one of the half dozen village halls on polling day.

Needless to say, there were some who deplored these high-powered tactics, comparing them to American presidential conventions, but on the whole people were grateful for this new diversion. It was not

that they had lost interest in Mr Waddington's iniquitous plans, simply that everything that could be said on the subject had
already been said several times over and
Avril's campaign had provided an unexpected fringe benefit. They could throw
themselves into it and lay bets on the outcome, without any feeling of disloyalty to
the cause.

One in particular who welcomed it was
Billy Jones, for he was greatly tickled by
the idea of Avril injecting new life, not to
mention the fear of God, into those complacent old-guard Councillors who had been
running the show for far too long. Also, in
supporting her campaign by word and deed,
he was able to regain his place in the best
of her books without any sacrifice of his
principles, with the added benefit of taking
some of the strain out of his relationship
with Miranda. Seeing which way the wind
was blowing, she took it as a sign that he
was coming round to her side although too
proud and stubborn to admit it, and had
chosen this means to show his repentance.

Mr Waddington's views on the matter
were not made known, but few could doubt
what form they would take and many were
convinced that he was behind the smear

campaign, whose salvo was fired in certain sections of the national press about a week before polling day.

It was not Avril but her husband who was the ostensible target and it started with two blow-ups of the same photograph appearing in two separate newspapers, showing the blurred figure of a man, who might or might not have been Robert, emerging from a London house which the caption of one described as the headquarters of the notorious Happy Days Club.

The story was taken up the following day by several other papers, one giving a potted biography of the subject, naming the various companies with which he was associated and the date when he had received his KBE from the Queen. The other carried an interview with Madame Elvira, the Club's proprietress, who spoke most warmly of Robert as a true and respected friend.

By this time too the telephone hardly stopped ringing from dawn to midnight and reporters were crawling round the house, with the declared intention of forcing themselves on Lady Avril, so that she could tell them whether she proposed to stand by her husband now that the scandal had been made public.

Naturally, she was more than capable of seeing them off with a few well-chosen words, but, heeding Robert's advice, remained indoors, incommunicado and a prisoner in her own house. Most of her well-chosen words, as he had pointed out, were liable to be unprintable, which would not deter anyone from printing them, thereby ruining her chances in the election.

It was sound advice, as far as it went, but only in the sense of shutting the stable door to keep a few more horses from bolting, for the first one had got away to a flying start and Avril's chances, if not in ruins, appeared to be severely dented. However, it did not seem to occur to either of them that without the initial indiscretion, none of it would have happened and fortunately neither of them had the sort of nature that dwelled on such trivialities. It was a development which had a profound effect on Billy, for although he considered himself entitled to criticise Avril as often as he saw fit, he would not tolerate a single word of censure from anyone else. Moreover, although he had no proof that Sam Waddington was responsible for this muck-raking exercise, he was left in no doubt as to the bitterness Waddington felt towards Avril and everything she stood for.

Chief Superintendent Wiseman, on the other hand, had felt curious enough to put out a few feelers regarding the source of these allegations. As a result, he discovered, soon after reaching his office the following morning, that the chairman of a company called Leisuredrome, which was heavily involved in the Upperfield development scheme, was also the owner of the two newspapers which had been the first to print them.

2

'Hope you won't mind riding in this old monster?' Rupert said later that day, when he called to collect Miranda for an evening out. 'It's not all that uncomfortable, so long as you don't mind being perched up a bit.'

'I don't mind in the least,' she told him. 'It won't be the first time, I assure you and I rather enjoy being perched up.'

All this was true and yet, oddly enough, the sight of him, so handsome, almost Byronic in Miranda's eyes, climbing out of a faintly familiar Land-rover instead of his own pale blue sports model, had brought a whiff of repugnance. It passed immediately and was soon forgotten, but at the time it had felt rather like biting into a shiny red cherry and finding it was made of wax.

'What have you done with your own car?' she asked when they had climbed aboard.

'Ruddy clutch has gone again. The garage promised to try and fix it by this evening, but nothing doing. So, rather than cancel our date, or take you on the bus to Brighton, I borrowed this from my Pa. Shall we go to the early show and have dinner after, or the other way round?'

Miranda, who liked to have everything in the right order, said, 'I don't mind, really, but when you said the clutch had gone again, did you mean that it happens all the time?'

Rupert did not reply at once and she was about to repeat the question when he said crossly, 'No, of course not, it's a marvellous car, but the way my old man was going on about it you'd imagine it did.'

'Why? Does he mind your borrowing this one?'

'On the contrary, pleased as Punch. That's why he was going on about it. Gave him the chance to bring out the boring old lecture about people who shoot around in fast dangerous cars, making a hideous racket and polluting the atmosphere to name but a few.'

'Doesn't sound very good, coming from a farmer.'

'Unfortunately, my love, he has a nasty way of practising what he preaches. One of his eccentricities is refusing to allow pesticides to be sprayed on his crops.'

'Well, good for him!'

'Yes, I thought you'd say that. It's not very good for business, though.'

'Does he really lose a lot by it?'

'About twenty-five per cent of the profits.'

'Gosh! No wonder he's got his knife into that rotten Waddington.'

They had stopped with a jerk behind another car at some traffic lights, which changed to amber while she was speaking and Rupert gave a series of blasts on the horn when the driver did not instantly move forward.

'Have I said something wrong?' Miranda asked, staring at his profile, a flickering memory stirring in the back of her mind.

'As though you could!' Rupert turned a smiling face towards her. 'No, it simply occurred to me that, in view of what happened to that effigy the other day, the sentiment might have been better expressed.'

'Oh yes, I see what you mean. Sorry about that,' Miranda muttered, dismayed by the way this was turning out to be such an inexplicably horrid evening. Some elusive recollection was still nagging at her. Rupert glanced at her with concern and slowed down.

'Why are you stopping?' she asked, as he pulled into a lay-by beside a bus stop.

'No special reason. I just felt the need to smother you with burning kisses. Any objection?'

After carrying out this ambition to the mutual satisfaction of both participants, Rupert said, 'I think it is high time I told the old man he is going to have a stunningly beautiful daughter-in-law' and all other thoughts evaporated from Miranda's mind.

Nine

Within a fortnight of his previous visit Geoffrey had found another reason to spend a night in London and this time he was proposing to drive there. His explanation was that on the last occasion he had bought two new suits, both requiring minor alterations, which were now ready for collection. He also intended to set himself up with some new shoes and a couple of shirts and did not relish the idea of carrying this extra load across London and on to the train.

Janet suggested that driving the car across London and finding somewhere to park it might also present difficulties to one so unfamiliar with the heavy traffic and the one-way systems, but he begged to differ. It appeared that he had been informed by the club porter of the existence of a small private car park at the back of the premises which was reserved for members who were stopping overnight.

'Naturally, it's entirely up to you, though,' he added. 'If it's going to inconvenience you to manage without the car for a couple of days, you have only to say so and I will make other arrangements.'

Janet automatically perjured herself by denying anything of the kind and nothing more was said on the subject for the rest of the day.

However, just before his departure on Monday morning she re-opened it a notch or two by saying, 'I've been thinking, Geoffrey. There may be one or two things I shall need from the shops tomorrow. Would it be possible for you to stop off and pick them up for me on your way home?'

'I foresee no difficulty. Just give me your list and it shall be done.'

'Well, the point is that I haven't made one yet, because it may not be necessary. I mean to ring up Lorna Bateman a little later on and, if she's going shopping either today or tomorrow, I know she'll give me a lift. So then there won't be any need to bother you with it. What I thought was that I could ring you up at the club between six and seven this evening and let you know. How would that be?'

'Most unsatisfactory in my opinion, and probably a waste of an expensive telephone call. How can I possibly tell you at this stage what time I shall be back at the club?'

'Well, in that case, I could leave a message for you to call me back when you do get in.'

'My dear Janet, all that trouble and expense just for the sake of a few groceries. I should have thought . . .'

'Oh well, never mind, I'll manage some other way. Forget I ever mentioned it.'

'But surely you could . . .'

'I said forget it, Geoffrey. It really doesn't matter in the least.'

And nor, in truth, did it, for she had only been using the shopping as a device to find out whether he really would be staying at his club or, as now seemed more probable, at 12, Sackville Court, Close or Crescent, in South-West London.

Suspicion turned to near certainty when Geoffrey telephoned on Tuesday morning to say that he would not be home until the following evening and she was tempted to throw caution, along with self-respect, to the winds by asking him whether, after all and given the right circumstances, he was made of money.

She restrained herself, however, and allowed him to plod on uninterrupted with the tale about one of the suits not having come up to scratch, so that further work had to be done on it and the longer he continued the less inclined she became to believe a single word.

There was also a practical side to the matter, which she found almost as humiliating as being fobbed off like a harmless imbecile and the object, no doubt, of great merriment for Jennifer and Geoffrey. Her new friend, Lorna Bateman, had suggested that the two of them should drive over to Brighton on Wednesday morning in her car, since she was familiar with all the parking dodges and one-way systems. Naturally, it had been Janet's intention to do the expected thing and invite her in for a drink before lunch when they returned. So now she was faced with having to invent some excuse for failing to do so, or else surreptitiously pick up a bottle of sherry during the shopping expedition and pray to God that Lorna wouldn't ask for a gin and tonic.

For the first time in her life she began to wonder what it would be like to be separated from Geoffrey, being her own mistress and this imaginary picture became still more alluring when he walked into the house late on Wednesday evening, carrying one small suitcase and a plastic bag containing the new shoes. He accounted for this by saying that he had managed to squeeze one of the suits in with the rest of his luggage and had left the other at his club. Since it was designed for formal wear only, there was no hurry about bringing it home.

Janet scarcely bothered to listen, her attention by this time having been diverted by a sideways view of a headline in the local paper, which he had collected from the post box when he came in and which stated 'Arson Suspected in Mystery Millionaire's Home'.

As soon as Geoffrey had gone upstairs for his wash and brush up before dinner, she gathered the paper into her lap and read the two paragraphs which followed this announcement. The information they contained would, in former times, have provided just the right ingredients for an interesting conversation at dinner and she was dying to talk to someone about it, but the warning voice which always sprang into action whenever that particular house was mentioned held her back and Geoffrey did not refer to it either.

This did nothing to lessen her resentment and on Thursday morning, while he was splashing about in the bathroom, she took her first bold step down the road to female emancipation by removing the drinks cupboard key from his pocket and putting it into her bag. Her plan was to take it, as soon as the coast was clear, to the While-U-Wait key grinder, which she had noticed when driving through the purlieus of Brighton the previous day.

However, when she came downstairs half

an hour later it was to discover that Geoffrey was not safely ensconced in the library and also that the car was not in the garage. They both returned soon after eleven, when he drove the car into the garage and remained there for a further thirty minutes.

This was mystifying, as well as frustrating and annoying, but although her curiosity and impatience were stretched to the limit, she did not go out and ask him what the hell he thought he was up to, feeling that this would be undignified and out of keeping with the mildly reproachful role she had been rehearsing all the morning.

The next time she saw him he was clipping the hedge in the front garden. This was quite unprecedented and although, in theory, no one was more delighted than she was to see the job done, it unnerved her almost more than anything that had gone before.

Punctually at ten to one, carrying two glasses and the sherry decanter and having stopped en route for the regulation wash and brush up, he arrived in the kitchen, where he had recently consented to eat his lunch when they were on their own.

'Well?' he asked when she did not speak.
'Well what, Geoffrey?'

'No praise, no congratulations? Not a word of thanks for all my hard labour?'

'Oh, you mean the hedge? Yes, I was very pleased to see you making a start on it at last. Especially as the mornings are usually sacred to your work.'

'Ah well, question of priorities, really. Seemed rather a waste to shut myself up indoors when we do get a fine day, for once. You agree?'

'Oh yes, very sensible. And I noticed the garden wasn't the only thing you spent time on this morning. I believe you took the car out for a couple of hours?'

'So I did, and that was another long over-due job. I took it down to the car wash. And then, for good measure, I came home and tidied out all that clutter in the boot. I can't imagine how it got into such a state.'

'And what did you do with all the clutter when you had removed it?'

'Put it into some cardboard boxes, which were also lying around, using up space. This afternoon, when I've finished the hedge, I'll make a bonfire and burn all the clippings as well. How's that for a good day's work?'

'Does this mean you've changed your mind about writing the book?'

'Good heavens, no, quite the reverse. But

I've discovered that you can't stick to the same routine every day and come fresh to it each time. Staleness is bound to creep in and I feel the book will be all the better for an occasional stint of hard labour in the fresh air.'

'In that case, Geoffrey, there's just one request I'd like to make.'

'And I shall do my best to grant it.'

'So, next time you feel this urge coming over you to take a break, would you be kind enough to give me advance notice when it involves taking the car out. It is going to be very difficult to run my life, not to mention the house, if I can never be certain of finding it in the garage when I need it.'

'Oh, certainly, although there could be no question of your needing it this morning. You told me only last night that, thanks to your expedition to Brighton, you had enough supplies to feed a regiment.'

'That's all very well, but, for all you knew, I might have had an appointment with the doctor or dentist this morning.'

'I consider it most unlikely that I should not have heard something about it, if you had. However, I accept the principle and I shall be careful to give you fair warning in future. I don't think you have much cause to worry,' he added, topping up his glass from the decanter. 'I daresay it will be quite a long time before I feel like spring cleaning the car again.'

And these, in Janet's view, were probably the truest words he had spoken for several days.

——Ten———————————————

1

The fire which had broken out at Uppfield Court on Monday night blazed on through most of Tuesday, incinerating the owner and effectively killing the story of Robert Meyer's fall from grace, although, to start with, the signs had pointed the other way.

The fact that two central characters lived within ten miles of each other was too lurid a coincidence to be resisted and for the first twenty-four hours both stories received equal coverage in the newspapers. None, however, went so far, except in the most roundabout way, to draw a connection between the two events and by the middle of the week Robert's name had ceased to appear at all.

By this time also it had become clear that Avril's campaign had actually received a shot in the arm from the Uppfield fire. Many voters, it seemed, took the view that, far from the need for a Councillor who would speak up for their interests having been wiped out by the removal of their principal adversary, the chances were that some yet more dangerous predator would now come along to replace him. Some even went so far as to say that their Independent candidate had already brought them luck and, given the opportunity, might well do so again.

On the following Thursday there was a larger than usual turn out at the polling stations, with the result that Avril cantered home with a sizeable majority.

By nine-thirty on Friday morning, while still at breakfast, Billy Jones had heard the news from Martha and was debating whether to telephone Avril to congratulate her when the doorbell rang.

'Ah!' he announced when he saw who the caller was. 'You have come to seek my views on some more funny goings-on at Uppfield Court?'

'Well yes, in a sense, I suppose I have. May I come in?'

'By all means. In fact, you are just in time for some coffee, if you don't mind drinking it in the kitchen.'

'It smells good,' Tubby said, seating himself at the scrubbed deal table, whose absence of clutter was a sure indication that Miranda was in residence. 'Were you expecting me?'

'Well, yes, in a sense, I suppose I was.'

'It's going to make a big difference to your life, I imagine? Your working life, that is?'

'Is that what you came to ask me?'

'Among other things.'

'Then I am sorry to say that I cannot give you the answer. It is certainly true that my work is now at a standstill, but whether the project will be revived and, if it is, whether I shall have any part to play in it is another question. I imagine that much depends on Waddington's heirs, whoever they may turn out to be. I daresay you are better informed on the subject than I am.'

'You didn't know that he had a wife?'

'No, I can't say I did. We never discussed personal matters, but they must have been separated for some years. Otherwise, it seems almost inevitable that she would have been mentioned at some point.'

'I take it you had not seen him for some

weeks? Not since his return from Barbados, perhaps?'

'No. So far as I was aware, he was in London during that time. Oddly enough, we had an appointment to meet at Uppfield last Monday, but he telephoned on Sunday evening to ask me to postpone it for a few days. Is there any connection between that question and the last one, or are we now following a new trail?'

'No, the same one, but before I explain, would you mind telling me what time this meeting was to have taken place?'

'He had invited me to lunch.'

'And did he give you any reason for wishing to postpone it?'

'Not that I recall. I believe he said something had come up, which is the second most meaningless sentence in the English language.'

'Oh, really? What's the first?'

' "We must meet for lunch one day". Do you usually go tripping round the maypole in this way when carrying out your investigations?'

'Not usually, but there is a logical sequence behind all this. I think that if he had not cancelled your lunch, or given a more specific reason for cancelling it, you would know more than you do about his wife.'

'That wouldn't be difficult, since I was unaware of her existence.'

'That is because, in that sense, it had only just begun. They were married at a Registrars in Kensington three days after his return from Barbados. I think it was a case of having the honeymoon before the wedding.'

'Who is she?'

'A young woman called Susannah Lennard. Ever met her?'

'I may have. He used to have parties down from London from time to time and most of the women were young.'

'You don't appear to be bowled over by the news.'

'No, nothing much surprises me these days and, as I've told you, his private concerns were no business of mine. I suppose this particular episode is likely to concern me in the future, though, since I assume she's the chief beneficiary?'

'Virtually the sole one. The new will was drawn up immediately after their marriage and he took the precaution of signing it before he left London last Sunday.'

'I wonder why she didn't come down here

with him? Oh, don't worry, I'm not intending to pry. I know you wouldn't tell me anything you don't consider fit for my ears and it will be less awkward for us both if I ask no questions.'

'The boot is on the other foot. I was hoping you might at least have met this young woman and be able to throw some light on their previous relationship. To tell you the truth, I can't quite make it out.'

'Have you asked her?'

'My Sergeant, Frank Ross, has. He had the job of going up to London to break the news. She'd heard about the fire by then, naturally, but at that point we didn't know whether Waddington was in the house or not. What remained of him wasn't found until several hours after the Fire Brigade reached the scene.'

'And what did Sergeant Ross make of her?'

'Not much on that occasion, apart from the bare facts. She was too distressed for anything more, although she managed to pull herself together to see him, having first of all absolutely refused to.'

'But Sergeant Ross did not discover why Waddington had abandoned her so early in their married life to go down to Uppfield on his own?'

'Yes, by degrees he did and the answer seemed reasonable enough. She had only expected him to be away for one night and, as he had urgent business to attend to, there would have been nothing for her to do except moon about on her own in an empty house. Furthermore, she would have been most uncomfortable, camping out, as it were, with no one to make up the fires or cook the dinner.'

'And presumably, of course, not even the fun of seeing it as her future home and making plans for decorating and so forth?'

'I suppose not, although I don't think that aspect of it was discussed. And, after all, you do seem to be asking most of the questions. Have you any more for me before I take my leave?'

'No, I don't think so. Oh well, just one, perhaps, although you may not see fit to answer it. Am I right in assuming that what we have here is a case of arson with murder thrown in?'

'My dear Bill, I thought better of you. Does that one really need an answer?'

'A sly one and no mistake, our Mr Jones,' he remarked later that day, when discussing the case with Frank Ross.

'Did you get the impression he was covering up?'

'I always get that impression with him, but that's not to say it's something incriminating, or even relevant. Concealment comes naturally to him and I've discovered that there's not much to be gained by trying to wear him down. Besides, he's hardly likely to have burnt the hand which fed him.'

'Although he might have some well-founded suspicions as to who did and be equally reluctant to pass them on?'

'Yes, he might, which is why I concentrated on handing out information, rather than trying to obtain it. When he's had time to think it over, he may decide to open up a bit. In the meantime, what have you got for me on the widow?'

'Not a great deal, as you see,' Frank replied, passing a page with three typed paragraphs across the desk.

'Age twenty-three,' Tubby said, reading aloud. 'First marriage four years ago. Divorced two years later and reverted to maiden name. No children. Anything known about the first husband?'

'Nothing much, except that she didn't set fire to him. Or, if she did, he survived. He married again soon after the divorce and now has twin daughters.'

'Whereas she remained single and there's no mention here of her having a job. Has she money of her own, or did she get a handsome settlement out of Number One?'

'I'm afraid it didn't occur to me to ask.'

'No, I suppose not.'

'I should think it might have been the second, though. She's pretty stunning looking and tough with it, I shouldn't wonder. Not the type to make the mistake of marrying a poor man.'

'That certainly wouldn't describe her second husband. Still, there's nothing to suggest that she was anywhere near Uppfield last weekend.'

'And also, surely if you were postulating the theory that she had somehow contrived his death, you'd have to admit that she'd have done much better to wait until the development plans had got the green light and the money was really starting to roll in?'

'Sorry to disagree, but I admit nothing of

the kind. If the plans do go through, any money that accrues to the present owner of the place will go straight into her bank account, whereas, if it's turned down, she still comes out the winner. She will be sole owner of the property and free to dispose of it in any way she chooses. Furthermore, removing her husband would have entailed far greater risks and complications once the house was sold and they were living together in London, instead of that isolated mausoleum, with only a bunch of hostile rustics on the perimeters.'

'It sounds as though you have already made up your mind that she is guilty?'

'No, I haven't done that either. I am simply trying to get it through to you that, in a case of this kind, where we have nothing at all to go on, it would be unwise to rule out any possibility, however seemingly far-fetched, until it has been tried and found wanting. I see no reason to write off the new Mrs Waddington just yet, but in the meantime what have you got for me on Ted and Alice Wilkes, son Gareth and the mystery of a newly-repaired jacket?'

'Well, starting with a brief re-cap, it began, as you remember on Easter Monday, with the anonymous telephone call.'

'Which was never traced?'

'No, though of course we were bound to take it seriously until proved wrong and, as it turned out, anyone seeing the dummy figure from outside the window could have mistaken it for human.'

'It would be interesting to know a bit more about that anonymous caller; but still, too late for that now. Go on.'

'The jacket and hat were put through all the routine tests, with negative results, the only item of interest being the note in a jacket pocket, the same one which Alice Wilkes had taken home to mend.'

'Which she claims was not there when she took it?'

'She could have been mistaken, though. It was wafer thin and weighed nothing at all. Also there was no reason for her to lie about it, since it's unlikely that it would have made any sense either to her or anyone in her family. Still more unlikely that one of them could have written it."

'Being in a foreign language. Greek, I think you said?'

'That was my first impression, based purely, I should add, on a holiday my wife and I spent in Corfu a year or two ago, but I must have been wrong. It was shown to an expert who confirmed that the script was Greek all right, but the words made no sense, so it must have been some ancient and remote country dialect. It didn't seem all that important at the time.'

'Naturally, since Waddington was still very much alive and kicking in Barbados. On reflection, did he show any sort of surprise or displeasure when you asked him about it?'

'Well, that was a strange thing, sir. He showed no surprise as such, in that I'd swear he had seen the note before. But something about it bothered him, I'm sure. Maybe he thought he had left it somewhere else or had thrown it away. Anyway he was a taciturn sort of man, as I'd always heard, and he just glanced at it, said something to the effect that it must have been in the pocket for months, then crumpled it up in an ashtray and set fire to it with his cigarette lighter.'

'Which could have been bad news, as things turned out, but fortunately you . . . Come on, Frank, don't be modest.'

'I'd had a photocopy made before we returned the original. I don't quite know why, except, I suppose the feeling that we couldn't afford to take any chances with a bigwig like him. Anyway, it's on the files and I'd like you to take a look at it some time.'

'Yes, I will. In the meantime, Frank, one thing becomes increasingly clear.'

'What is that, sir?'

'Whether or not the mock murder and the real one were committed by the same hand, whoever dreamt up the first certainly managed to bring the proposed corpse back to the scene of the crime and in the process threw several layers of confusion over the second murder, just to obscure the picture. Now about Mrs Wilkes and the jacket . . .'

——Eleven——

1

A week later the plans for the re-development of the Uppfield estate, details of which had then been on view to the general public for three months, were formally submitted for approval by the Planning Committee and, after a long and heated argument, were turned down by a majority of three to two.

There could be no doubt that this outcome owed much to the forthright and well argued submission of the Independent member, although perhaps having less to do with the speech Robert had prepared for her than the standing which they both enjoyed in the local community. The majority of the Council members were old established business and professional people who, as eager as the next man to enlarge their business and professional activities by whatever means were on offer, were also aware of the disadvantages which could accrue to themselves, not to mention their wives and families, by getting on the wrong side of Avril Meyer, whose estate was even larger and voice a hundred times more powerful than that of the late Sam Waddington.

This triumph for the opposition was short lived, however, and amounted, in effect, to no more than a breathing space in which to re-group their forces, for a few days later it was rumoured that the developers were to appeal against the ruling, having hired the most wily, sought-after and experienced QC in the land to plead their case at the next public hearing.

Many of the wiser and more experienced heads in the community had anticipated this move and had already taken some steps towards foiling it. Unfortunately, though, the net profits from the Bring-and-Buy parties,

Sponsored Walks and Car Boot Sales still amounted to less than three thousand pounds, or scarcely a fifth of what would be needed to obtain the services of the second most wily and sought-after Counsel for the Defence.

When the message sank in the crusading spirit which had shone so brightly became dampened almost overnight, to be replaced by a mixture of frustration and disillusionment. It was unlikely that many of those concerned had actually prayed for someone to come along and murder Mr Waddington and they did not light beacons on the Downs or rejoice openly when it came about, but most had probably uttered a silent word of thanks. The realisation that the fight would go on, with or without him, was an outcome they had been unprepared for.

It was not altogether satisfactory for Avril either because, by an annoying paradox, so far as any practical assistance went she might as well have now had both hands tied behind her back. Had she still been a private citizen, she would have dealt with the problem, or at any rate got the counter-attack off to a blazing start by revealing that the picture she had sent for auction in London had fetched four times its estimated price, or some such farrago, and handing the balance over to the treasurer of the anti-development trust. However, such trickery was now quite ruled out by her election to the Council and no amount of cleverly written speeches by Robert could absolve her from charges of bribery and corruption if the truth came out.

Complaining about this situation to Martha, she said, 'I suppose you wouldn't be game for a bit of money laundering?'

'I might, I suppose, if I knew what it meant.'

'Quite simply, the idea is that I pay some money into your account and you put it around that it's a legacy from your aunt and that you felt it would be in accordance with her wishes to hand it over to the anti-development fund.'

Martha weighed up this suggestion, less from the moral than the practical aspect. 'I'm afraid it wouldn't work, you know, Avril. I mean, people might just swallow the idea that I had an aunt, my father's youngest sister, perhaps, and that she thought highly enough of me to leave me her money, although they might think it strange that they'd never seen or heard of her. The hard part would be to convince them that I'd choose to use it in that way, when they all know that I haven't got two pennies to rub together and haven't any idea how I'm going to be able to afford to get the roof repaired.'

Avril sighed. 'Yes, I expect you're right. Everyone thinks you're a saint, of course, but I suppose even you wouldn't take it to those lengths. I shall have to think of something else.'

Martha was silent for a while and then she said, 'I'm not sure I'd bother, if I were you.'

'Oh, you mustn't be defeatist.'

'It's not that, but the situation has changed since we first started parading with our banners and organising protest marches.'

'In what way has it changed?'

'Well, you remember how easy it was in those days to get people on our side?'

'Except Billy, of course.'

'Yes, except Billy, but in general the cause was taken up by virtually everyone for miles around. All the ecologists and conservationists were out in force, which was only to be expected, but we also got support from the weekenders and people who had no roots here at all and no special interest in preserving the countryside, because they could always pull out and move somewhere else. All that worried them was the value of their property going down and having to sell it for less than they'd paid, if the plans went through.'

'Yes, I've no illusions about them. What of it?'

'They are finding out their mistake. It seems that prices around here have been shooting up during the past few months. No, really, Avril, I know it sounds absurd, but for once I do know what I'm talking about. When I said just now that I was bothered about how to pay for the roof, it was no joke and a few weeks ago I nerved myself to ask my bank manager whether he'd consider letting me have an overdraft. He told me that a better way to do it might be to take out a mortgage on the house.'

'My dear Martha, why ever didn't you tell me? I had no idea things were so dicey.'

'You know very well why I didn't tell you, so let's not go into that. I only mention it now because it has a bearing on what we've been talking about. The first thing I had to do, you see, was to get a surveyor to go over the place with a toothcomb, so I rang up the estate agents and young Mr Aldringham, who's married now, with two children, believe it or not, spent a whole day jabbing pins into walls and taking up floorboards. He told me afterwards that his firm could probably get a quarter of a million for it, just as it stands. Don't you find that perfectly ridiculous?'

'Yes, of course I do, but, as Robert would tell you, it's only on paper. If you were to sell it and move into something smaller, you'd only have to pay a lot over the odds for it.'

'I realise that and I'm hoping it won't be necessary, but what you say only applies to properties in this area. If, for the sake of argument, I was willing to spend my declining years in Lincolnshire, for instance, just think how well off I should be.'

'And did young Mr Aldringham explain why our houses have become so much more valuable?'

'Yes, he did and, believe it or not, we have Mr Waddington to thank for it. It seems that property round here is now among the most sought after in the whole country.'

'So I gather, Martha, but why?'

'Because to an awful lot of people it is about to offer the best that life can provide.

The village itself won't be affected and what do they care about the dewponds being bull-dozed out of existence and turned into putting greens? What matters to them is having supermarkets, cinemas and golf courses right on their doorstep, with none of the hassle of driving to Brighton or Lewes and wasting hours crawling round looking for a parking space. That's what we're up against.'

'Well, it sounds bleak, I admit, but there's still a glimmer of hope.'

'I'd be interested to hear what it is.'

'The programme, we're told, is for the consortium, or whatever they call them-selves, to go ahead with their plans, with or without the ghastly Waddington, but you've overlooked an important point. No specu-lator, however powerful, can develop land without the consent of the owner and no-body knows yet who does own Uppfield now. He or she may have quite different ideas and decide to leave things exactly as they are.'

'I hadn't thought of that,' Martha ad-mitted. 'I'd assumed he'd already sold it to these people, but I suppose he wouldn't have been able to do that until he'd got building permission. So now everything depends on the new owner. I do wish we knew who it was.'

'You're not the only one,' Avril assured her.

2

The same topic was at that moment exercising the mind of Superintendent Wiseman, for he had just received some unexpected news. Frank Ross had arrived in his office a few minutes earlier to report on his second interview with Mrs Waddington, and Tubby had begun by asking whether she was now ready to be a little more forthcoming about her husband's death.

'I wouldn't go as far as that. She complained a bit about the delays and inefficiency of the fire services, but she also admitted that Waddington himself may have been partly to blame for what happened.'

'How so?'

'She said he was incurably careless about that sort of risk. Always leaving taps running and lighted cigars on the rim of ashtrays, which then fell off and burnt holes in the carpet. He even did that in bed, apparently.'

'She didn't happen to mention that he was also in the habit of leaving piles of straw and rags soaked in paraffin at the foot of the staircase and chucking a lighted cigar on them?'

'Is that how it started?'

'Something on those lines. What else did you get? Was she able to tell you anything about this business appointment he had down here on Monday?'

'Up to a point, although she assured me that her opinion was only based on surmise and I don't know how much reliance should be put on it. The only thing is, I can't see any reason why she should have made it up.'

'So what did she surmise?'

'That it most likely had something to do with his decision to pull out of the development project. She thinks he must have called this meeting of colleagues and confederates for the express purpose of breaking it to them.'

'Well, I'm damned. Why has she kept it so quiet all this time?'

After a pause the Sergeant said, 'Well, I'm sorry to tell you, sir, that the simple answer is that I didn't ask her. She went on to say that she realised now that she ought to have mentioned it before, but since it hardly seemed possible that it could have any connection with the fire she saw no reason to discuss his private affairs, which concerned no one but themselves. All quite true, no doubt, but it didn't make me feel any better.'

'Did she give you any reason for this change of heart?'

'Just that it was her idea, in the first place and she'd talked him into it. She'd told him that she didn't see any point in destroying the environment and alienating the community they were proposing to live in just to make more money, when they had plenty to live comfortably on without it. If things didn't work out, they could still go ahead with the conversion plans for the big house and move into a smaller place themselves. One way and another, she had it all so cut and dried that I found it hard to believe she'd made it up on the spur of the moment and, as I say, what did she have to gain by it? All the same, I could easily be wrong and I think it might be a good idea if you were to have a talk with her yourself.'

'Yes, perhaps I should, but in the meantime, Frank, I see no reason for you to reproach yourself. Mrs Waddington may well have thought it would be a bright idea to achieve a little glory for herself by laying claim to these noble, high-flown sentiments as all her own unaided work, now that there is no one left to say her nay. On the other hand, it would be equally plausible to suggest that it had dawned on Waddington that the joker with the dummy corpse meant business and he was beginning to get cold feet about the whole affair. Either way, you see where it lands us?'

'Pretty much where we were before, I suppose?'

'Oh no, worse than that. It pulls the rug from under our feet. We had precious little to go on, as it was, but at least we could narrow the field down to those with a strong motive and, for once, the motive stood out a mile. It announced itself plainly as someone who would go to extreme lengths to prevent the development plans from going through. That's all washed up now.'

'Not necessarily, surely? Very few people could have known at that time that he'd changed his mind, if indeed he had.'

'Enough, in theory anyway, to knock our case flat on its face. If he'd gone to the trouble of calling a special meeting to announce that he was changing course, there's a good chance that those in the know would already have guessed which way the wind was blowing. The obvious thing at this point would have been for our man to have held his hand, until he knew how matters would turn out.'

Having pondered this for a moment or two, Frank suggested, 'So why not turn the picture round and look at it from the other way up? Supposing, for the sake of argument, that someone in Waddington's circle did know of his intentions and had a lot to lose by it. With so much money at stake, I suppose that could have been a pretty powerful incentive?'

'Except that such an individual could only have been involved with Waddington in a purely business sense. Anyone who knew him well personally, would have been aware that his death would solve nothing, so long as his wife remained alive. On the other hand, of course, we now have to take into the account that even if she was speaking the truth when she told you she had been the one who was against selling out to the developers, she could well be excused for changing her mind now. Uppfield might have had its attractions as a home for a married couple, with hopes perhaps of raising a family, but not much cop for a lonely widow. And, of course, if she should decide to sell it, she won't be in a position to lay down conditions as to what the purchaser does with it. Incidentally, I take it the house was adequately insured?'

'More than that. The cover was increased by getting on for fifty per cent at the same time as he made his new will. That's one reason why the insurance companies have had their assessors out in force, crawling through the rubble. Naturally, they see the fire as rather a heavy coincidence.'

'Ah well, I daresay it won't bankrupt them. And they're forever bombarding the rest of us with warnings about being under-insured, so it's only fair if they're the ones to be caught for once. What were we saying before that?'

'That what we're now lumbered with is a murderer who either didn't know about Waddington's change of plans and wanted to put a major spanner in the works, or who did know and was dead set on making sure that the developers got their way. Fine old mish-mash, isn't it, sir?'

'An apt description and, so far as I can

see, it brings us smartly back to square one, minus one.'

3

The same elements of frustration and uncertainty were prevalent in other areas too. From her new eminence, Avril was able to reveal that so far there had been no indication that an appeal was to be lodged against the Council's veto and when the inquest on Sam Waddington opened on Monday morning it was promptly adjourned for an indefinite period, pending further investigations. These, in the general, as well as in the official view, were likely to take months rather than weeks and, furthermore, the local population was to be denied so much as a glimpse of the widow. The announcement in the obituary columns merely stated that the cremation, which many considered to be superfluous in the circumstances, would be private, with family flowers only.

'So not exactly a bower of roses and lilies there,' Avril remarked to Billy Jones, when they met in the post office, 'seeing that, so far as anyone knows, until this wife turned up he didn't possess any family at all.'

'I believe there were a few cousins scattered about in the North,' he replied, 'but I doubt if they'll bother to attend. They certainly wouldn't have much to gain by it. I see that you're allowed to park anywhere you choose, now that you're a Councillor,' he added, as they moved out to the main road, where Avril's car stood in lonely state on a stretch of double yellow lines.

'Not at all. I had a couple of mountainous parcels to send off and no one would expect a woman of my age to lug them all the way from the car park. Where's yours?'

'Oh, I walked.'

'Hop in then and I'll give you a lift home.'

When they were on their way she asked, 'Would you mind stopping off for a moment at our house first? Miranda lent me a book, which I've been meaning to return for weeks. We could have a snifter while I dig it out.'

'What's it called?' he asked. 'Not *The Olive Branch*, by any chance?'

'Something like that, I expect. I couldn't make head or tail of it, if you want to know, but no need to pass that on.'

'I sympathise. I am finding all forms of

communication with Miranda heavy going at present.'

'Oh well, inevitable, I suppose.'

'I don't see why. I may not always have been the most unselfish parent in the world and naturally I accept that there are some subjects she couldn't discuss with me as she would have with her mother, if she'd had the misfortune to know her. I imagine that in an odd sort of way Martha has come closest to filling that gap. But she is an uninhibited girl as a rule and we've never lacked topics for discussion. All that seems to have changed during the past few weeks.'

'And can you wonder, Billy, seeing that the principal topic of conversation for all of us for the past few weeks has been the one on which you and Miranda are dug in on opposing lines?'

'My dear Avril, if you're referring to Waddington and his development plans, you're several miles wide of the mark. For one thing, that has been going on for months, not weeks and, for another, it happens to be the one subject on which Miranda has always been at her most vociferous. She has never missed an opportunity to state her own views and nag me about mine. This is something else. Being in love, perhaps, although I find that surprising too. I had always believed it to be a situation in which girls are all too anxious to unburden themselves to anyone who will listen.'

'If your theory about Martha is right, she may know what's behind it. Why don't you ask her?'

'Thank you, but I don't consider that to be very constructive advice.'

'Oh, you're so proud, aren't you, Billy? It will get you into trouble one of these days. The poor child's head over heels with young Rupert Crossman; anyone can see that. I expect you said something heavy-fatherish about him which hurt her feelings. Though why you should object to having that young man as your future son-in-law is beyond me. He is *very* eligible, if you ask me, and nice with it,' Avril said, sweeping round the drive with great verve and speed and slamming to a stop outside her imposing front door.

A bit too eligible, if you ask me, thought Billy, and the trouble was that nobody had.

Twelve

1

'Well, goodness knows, Miranda,' Martha was saying, 'I'm not advocating spinster-hood as the ideal life for a woman, but I should have thought that anything would be preferable to marrying someone because you couldn't bear to hurt his feelings by showing him the door.'

'It's not as simple as that, Martha.'

'I hardly thought it could be, but since you say you want my opinion, perhaps it would be a good idea to tell me what the trouble really is.'

'I'm afraid the boot might be on the other foot.'

'Meaning that he's changed his mind about wanting to marry you and can't bear to hurt your feelings?'

'I know it must sound daft, but I suppose in my heart that's exactly what I do believe. I haven't changed, but I think he has and I'm too much of a coward to ask him straight out. I suppose you think I should?'

'On the contrary, I'm sure you're exaggerating the whole thing and making far too much of it.'

'Honestly, Martha, how can you possibly say that when you haven't even met him?'

'No, I haven't and I also admit I'm not in any way qualified to play Miss Lonelyhearts. All the same, I must tell you that over the years it has come to my notice that the average young man, especially if he happens to be well off and endowed with looks and charm, tends not to be quite so delicate in these matters as the average young woman. You may find this cynical, but I have a strong suspicion that if he had changed his mind about wanting to marry you he would have had no trouble in finding a way to let you know and blow your feelings!'

'Yes, okay, but supposing that's just what he's been trying to do and I'm so thick that the message hasn't got through to me?'

'Oh, I doubt it. He's not some shy, shambling youth, you know. He's been spoilt rotten by his father, so they say, and everything he's asked for has been dumped in his lap. Something tells me that if the message hadn't got through to you straight away he'd have found some other way to make it clear.

Anyway, what makes you feel he's cooling off?'

'Oh, just small things, really, but they mount up. We just don't seem to be on the same wavelength any more. For example, one of the first things we discovered we had in common was being only children and not having really known our mothers. It made a sort of bond and the other day I said, in a sort of jokey way, that we'd make up for being so deprived by having at least five children and being devoted parents. I wasn't being serious, but he suddenly rounded on me as though I'd said something really offensive and disgusting. It was so unexpected that it gave me a shock and the trouble is that there've been several of those completely irrational outbursts since then and I'm getting to the stage where I hardly dare open my mouth.'

It was beginning to sound to Martha as though the root of Miranda's problem was that she had fallen for a conceited and humourless oaf and would be better off without him, but realising that there would be no comfort in this she said, 'Do you think he has something on his mind, which he feels uncomfortable or ashamed about and that's why he hits out at you sometimes? If

155

so, from what I hear about it, you are getting good training for married life.'

'I don't see why he wouldn't be able to confide in me, whatever it is. He must know I'd be on his side and, anyway, he never used to be like this before. I can't see how anything can have happened since to make him feel bothered or ashamed because we either meet or telephone each other practically every day.'

'So when did you first notice this change in him?'

'Can't put an exact date on it, but it must have been around the time when Avril got on to the Council. There were some other people there when we were talking about it and one of them was saying what a bit of luck it was and how we could all now sit back and leave it to her to see off ghastly people like Mr Waddington and then I . . .'

'So this obviously was before the fire at Uppfield?'

'Must have been; or, at any rate, before any of us realised that there'd been anyone there when it happened, because I said something about how I hoped Avril wouldn't have to resort to arson very often and Rupert flew at me and more or less told me to stop being a fool and shut up. It was really embarrassing.'

'Yes, it must have been, but it sounds to me as though it was all this talk about the fire which made him burst out like that, nothing to do with you, personally.'

'It bloody well sounded personal to me and to everyone else who heard it. And, anyway, why should Uppfield going up in flames affect him like that? He'd never been inside the place in his life and he hardly knew Mr Waddington.'

'No, of course not, but I was thinking . . . well, more of his father.'

'What's he got to do with it?'

'Well, it's like this, you see, Miranda. I don't know Mr Crossman at all well, but there are people who do and almost the first thing most of them would be able to tell you about him was this bee he had in his bonnet about Mr Waddington. You've heard the story yourself, I daresay?'

'Yes, of course, I have, but that was all over years and years ago. I can't see why anyone should bother to get excited about it now. Anyone but him, that is. Oh, now hold on, I believe I see what you're driving at. You're hinting that Rupert has now got hold of the idea that after all these years his father has got his revenge at last by burning Uppfield to the ground and making sure the hated enemy was inside when he did it. Is that it?'

'No, certainly not. All I'm suggesting is that this is what the politicians call a sensitive area and it could well be that Rupert, for whom the whole sad business has loomed so large ever since he was a child, is afraid that some malicious person will make the connection, even if they don't voice it aloud, and this is what makes him so touchy. Everything will blow over and get back to normal when they find out who really did start the fire. Just you wait and see.'

'The snag there, according to my Dad, is that we're likely to be old and grey, if not pushing up the daisies, by the time that happens.'

'Oh, Billy's always been a pessimist, you shouldn't take too much notice of him. Tubby may not go about things in a very spectacular way or have a passionate interest in anything much except the creature comforts, but he's very clever really and very patient and he's sure to get his man in the end. We shall just have to do all we can to make sure he keeps on the right lines.'

Miranda was far too involved in her own problems to ponder how a middle-aged spinster would keep a Superintendent of the police on the right lines, and forgot the words as soon as they had been uttered.

2

One who did not share Martha's confidence about his chances of emerging victorious from the conflict was Superintendent Wiseman.

'We seem to be getting nowhere rather slowly,' he remarked to Frank Ross. "I trust you have something interesting to report on your activities over the past twenty-four hours?'

'I'm afraid it does nothing to break the deadlock, sir, if that's what you were hoping.'

'It was, but I'd better hear the bad news.'

'Taking into account your reminder that criminals tend not to be an imaginative breed, plus the other well-known fact that members of the Wilkes family had the best motive and opportunity for committing both crimes, I paid a second visit to Millpond Farm this morning.'

'What time was that?'

'Just after midday.'

'And Ted was at home?'

'No, I was sure he wouldn't be and had taken the precaution of leaving the car out in the lane, in the expectation that he would come in for his dinner via the yard entrance and discover me in situ, as it were. In the meantime, it was a chance to have a little chat with Alice on her own.'

'And was she on her own?'

'No, her sister, Edna Bailey, was there. You know her, I'm sure? They were making lemon curd and I was given a jar to take home with me.'

'Well, that's something, I suppose. Did you get anything else out of it?'

'Nothing as useful as that, I'm afraid. I explained that we were trying to pinpoint the time when the fire had started and asked her exactly when she or her husband had first noticed it. She said she couldn't speak for Ted because he'd gone out to see to the milking before she was up. The first she'd known about it herself was seeing this great cloud of smoke, when she was out collecting the eggs, at about eight o'clock. She keeps a couple of dozen hens and sells the surplus eggs as a sideline. She knew it couldn't have been after eight because she has a regular customer who calls every Monday after she's dropped her husband off at the station. When she'd been, Alice went back up to her room and, seeing it from above, as you might say, realised that the cloud of smoke must be coming from that hollow where Uppfield Court stands because normally on a clear day like that one you'd be able to see the chimneys and part of the roof. Soon after that Ted had come in for his breakfast and after they'd talked it over for a bit they decided there'd have been other people nearer the spot, who'd have reported it by then, so there was nothing much they could do about it. All the same, as soon as he'd finished his breakfast, Ted said he'd get down there and see whether there was anything he could do. As a result, then and then only, was the Fire Brigade alerted.'

'And was Ted able to add anything to this dull and blameless version of events?'

'I didn't hang around long enough to ask him. He hadn't come back by the time we'd been through all this, so perhaps he'd caught sight of my car after all and decided his dinner could wait. And I doubt if it made any difference. Alice had got it all off so pat that you may be sure they'd agreed in advance exactly what they'd say and nothing short of a thunderbolt would have changed it.'

'You'd been prepared for something like this, I take it?'

'Yes, but I felt it was worth having a shot at breaking them down. They'd been asked these questions, or similar ones before, although not by me, and there was just a chance that one of them, Alice in particular, realising we weren't going to let it drop, might fall into the trap of embroidering a little, in the hope of making it sound more convincing.'

'But you got nothing for your pains by the sound of it and that door remains as firmly closed as ever?'

'There was just one crumb, which might be worth passing on to you,' Frank said. 'Towards the end, when I'd been chatting them up a bit in a general way, Edna came out with the news that Miss Kershaw, the lady she goes to twice a week, was of the opinion, unlike you and me, that there wasn't likely to be any connection between the fire and the planting of the dummy figure which had turned up in the dining room a few weeks earlier. Of course, I realised that it was in the Wilkes's interest to bring us round to this view, but it seemed odd that she should expect us to do so on such flimsy evidence as that. So I asked whether Miss Kershaw had offered any explanation for her theory and what do you suppose her answer to that was?'

'Having some acquaintance with the lady and the workings of her mind, I should not be so rash as to hazard a guess.'

'She claimed to have a shrewd idea of who had been responsible for the effigy and, if she was right, it was someone who couldn't possibly have set fire to the house.'

'She didn't by any chance name him? No, I thought not. Still, I suppose we're obliged to follow it up.'

'Want me to call on Miss Kershaw, sir?'

'No, perhaps not, Frank. All things considered, it might be best to take this one on myself.'

——Thirteen——

1

'Good morning, Martha. I hope this isn't an inconvenient moment to call?'

'Oh, hello, Tubby, do come in. Everything's in a bit of a mess, I'm afraid. There hasn't been time to tidy up yet and Mrs Bailey doesn't come on Mondays.'

'Well, don't worry,' he said, having already made sure of this. 'It shouldn't take very long.'

'Oh dear, now you're making it sound like an official call.'

'I'm afraid it is, in a way. The fact is, Martha, I hear you've been holding out on us.'

'I suppose that means Mrs Bailey has been spreading tales?'

'Was it just a tale?'

'Not altogether, but she wasn't supposed to pass it on to you,' Martha replied, speaking in rather a gabble, but with less than her usual hesitancy, having rehearsed this part of the script. 'After all, it was only my personal view and, in any case, rigging up a dummy corpse and leaving it in someone's dining room is probably not a very serious crime.'

'Nevertheless, it might have some bearing on a very serious one which occurred soon afterwards and, personal or not, your opinion was presumably based on some kind of evidence. Why don't we sit down while you tell me about it?'

'Oh, very well. Would you like some coffee?'

'Not at the moment, thank you. I'd like to get this cleared up first. Now, am I right in believing that you told Mrs Bailey that you knew who had planted the dummy?'

'Not that I knew for certain. How could I, without being a witness to the deed itself? Only that everything pointed to one man.'

'Whose name is?'

'I'm afraid I can't tell you.'

'Well, that's not a very good start.'

'I know, but what I can tell you is that until a few weeks ago he and his wife used to be the cook and gardener at Uppfield.'

'You mean the couple who lived at the Lodge?'

'Yes. The story goes that Mr Waddington kept them on as long as he did because the wife was such a paragon, but the man was a dead loss, who never drew a sober breath and he finally gave them the push just before he left for Barbados. Well, according to Mrs Bailey, who brings me all the gossip, during the week they were under notice this man used to spend all his time in the local pubs threatening to bring charges of wrongful dismissal and swearing vengeance on his ex-employer. Had you heard about that?'

'They're a couple called Wicker and I must say I'd hoped you would come up with something a little more concrete than vague rumours of that kind.'

'And so I will. Just cast your mind back to Easter Sunday and Avril's lunch party. During lunch Billy had been talking about the plan to divide Uppfield up into separate houses. It was the first time I'd heard him talk openly on the subject, even to that extent, and you'll also remember that the rather nice woman who was at lunch too, Gillford I think she was called, had seemed quite keen on the idea of her and her husband moving into one of them.'

'It seemed to me that she was rather more keen than he was.'

'Oh, you pick up all the nuances, don't you, Tubby? Well, anyway, enough was said to make me feel curious about it myself, so, just on impulse, I went on to Uppfield and parked my car by the Lodge gates.'

'Whatever for? It's at least three-quarters of a mile walk from there.'

'I had a special reason for leaving the car at the top.'

'Well, tell me what it was. Every little helps, one imagines.'

'One thing I did remember about Uppfield from the few times I'd been there before was that the house stands all on its own in a hollow and that the drive down to it is only single track most of the way and once you've started you can't turn round and go back till you get to the bottom. It was no part of my plan to land up outside the front door. There might have been someone there, or Mr Waddington might have come home unexpectedly, which is something I gather he's rather apt to do. Anyway, to continue with the saga, I'd been walking for about twenty minutes through the trees on the left of the drive, where you get a clear view of the house from about half way down, and I decided that it was a gloomy old place and nothing on earth would persuade me to live there. So I turned round and started back up again.'

Realising that he would only make matters worse by begging her to come to the point, Tubby nodded and waited for her to continue, which she did by saying, 'It was a good thing I had decided to walk because when I was nearly at the top a car came by from the direction of the house, so if I'd taken mine I should have been caught red-handed.'

'Could you see who was driving?'

'No, only that it was a man. It was too far off for anything more, but the next time I saw the car it was parked outside the Lodge and I concluded it must belong to someone whose job it was to keep a check on the place and make sure it hadn't been broken into and so on. But then afterwards I realised that couldn't possibly be the answer. It was Easter, after all, with the Boss away on the other side of the Atlantic. It wasn't very likely that anyone would be as conscientious as all that. That was when I got the idea that it was most likely the man, what did you say his name was? Yes, Wicker, revisiting old haunts, although I didn't see anything sinister about it at the time.'

'But later, when you heard about the mock corpse, you assumed without question that he'd been responsible?'

'Well, after all, why not, Tubby? He must have been up to some mischief because there was no sign of a car anywhere near the big house when I was looking down on it. So that means he'd gone to the trouble of parking it somewhere out of sight, maybe in the garage, for all I know. That's what makes me sure it was Wicker. He was one of the few people from outside who would have known about Mr Waddington being in Barbados and that there'd be no domestic staff around at a weekend. He'd also have been familiar with all the ways of getting into the house and switching the burglar alarm off before it rang in the police station. And who else would have possessed a key to the Lodge?'

'Although he didn't make any secret about that part of it, did he? Just walked in, leaving the car outside for anyone to see. What would he have done if someone, Billy Jones, for instance, had turned up and decided to investigate? Come to that, if his business was down at the house, why did he need to take the unnecessary risk of stopping off at the Lodge at all?'

'Well, I can't be expected to see into his mind, can I? Perhaps he wanted to go to the bathroom or something, but it's possible that they'd left some of their possessions behind and he'd come back to retrieve them. At any rate, I know that's what I'd have said if I'd been caught in the act, and I'd also have thrown in something about having taken the keys by mistake and using this chance to return them.'

'I don't suppose it occured to you to make a note of the car registration number?'

'No, why should it? It was an ordinary old blue or grey thing, like you see dozens of every time you go out, but, apart from that, I hardly gave a thought to the whole episode. It was really no business of mine what went on at Uppfield and only afterwards, when we heard what had happened at the house, did I realise it must have been this Wicker I saw and that's what he'd been up to.'

'But you still said nothing about it?'

'No, there didn't seem much point. Nobody had been hurt, nothing in the house damaged or stolen and if ex-employees wanted to go around playing malicious jokes on their former employers, who was I to interfere? Besides, what use would it have been if I had told you? I never came face to face with the man, so I couldn't have identified him and you may be sure that no one else in those parts got a close look either. Apart from a few cyclists and ramblers, the whole place was deserted.'

'Nevertheless, you have told me now, so what made you change your mind?'

Martha remained silent for a moment or two, looking down at her hands, as though interested to find they belonged to her, a trick which Tubby had noticed before in people he was interviewing. Finally she said, 'I've been expecting you to ask me that and it's rather hard to explain. It had never occured to me, you see, that the two events, the straw dummy and the fire, were connected, in that the same person must have been responsible for both. But then someone pointed out that it was too much of a coincidence that two entirely separate people should have been involved and his theory was that the first one was a threat of something more serious to come, unless Mr Waddington mended his ways. In other words, that he risked his life by carrying on with his shoddy development plans; but either the message eluded him, or else he decided to call their bluff and that's why the house was burnt down. So that's when I decided I ought to tell you everything I knew about the first incident, even though I couldn't prove it.'

'Yes, I see and I'm glad you have. No telling whether it will lead anywhere, but many a mickle makes a muckle, as we say in the trade and it will certainly have to be followed up.'

What he did not tell Martha was that Uppfield Court and its owner had been eliminated despite, it seemed, Mr Waddington heeding the message of the dummy and abandoning his shoddy development plans.

Judging the effective part of the interview to have been completed, Tubby heaved himself up from his chair before the social part could begin. Sure enough, there was Martha offering coffee.

'No, thanks, Martha,' he replied. 'I'd like to, but I'd better not stop. Frank's waiting for me and we're on our way to London. However, if I might just use your telephone before I go? Something I forgot to see to before I left my office.'

'Yes, of course. You know where it is?'

'In the kitchen, I believe, although I've never been able to understand why.'

'Because that's where I always seem to be whenever anyone takes it into their head to ring up.'

'Ah well, that explains everything,' he agreed, getting up and going out of the room, without closing the door behind him.

2

'Three o'clock, our next appointment, is that right?' he asked, as they circled round Clapham Common.

'Right, sir. I tried to make it earlier, but it seems her doctor has prescribed an hour's rest every afternoon, while she recovers from the shock.'

'In that case, you can drop me off somewhere near Burlington House. There are one or two things I can see to while I'm here and I'll get a glass of wine and something to eat at my club. How long will it take us to get from there to Park Street?'

'Not more than twenty minutes, I should say.'

'Then pick me up at half past two. In the meantime, Frank,' he added, taking a folded sheet of paper from his pocket, 'see what you can do with this as a first step in tracking down the Wickers. It appears that we don't have any home address for them on the files, but this is the name of the agency who hired them out to Waddington.'

'You didn't get it from Miss Kershaw, by any chance?'

'No, and I thought the less she knew about it the better. Fortunately, for all her funny ways, she is not one to listen in to other people's telephone conversations.'

'But you do consider her story to be worth following up? Not just another example of her funny ways?'

'I haven't formed an opinion one way or the other yet, but it would seem that we can't afford to let any stones lie around unturned.'

Frank made no comment, his full attention now being needed to make a right-hand turn into a side street of Piccadilly.

'This do you all right, sir?' he asked, having completed the manoeuvre.

'Splendidly, thank you, Frank,' Tubby replied, extricating himself from the passenger seat on to the pavement by the side entrance to Fortnum and Mason.

Guy Kenton was standing by the bar, talking to another man when Tubby arrived at his club. Kenton, now retired and living in great style, so it was said, somewhere near Henley-on-Thames, with his own vineyard and helicopter and a Chinese wife who rarely appeared in public, had formerly been a stockbroker on the Singapore Exchange. During his working life, however, he had made regular and prolonged visits to London and over the years Tubby had formed a close acquaintance with him, on the whole finding both his company and his anecdotes more stimulating than those of the London-based stockbrokers, civil servants and lawyers, who made up the bulk of the membership.

His companion on this occasion was also immediately recognisable, causing him to say when he and Guy joined up for lunch, 'That chap you were talking to in the bar, you know him well?'

'Used to. Fellow called Gillford. Hadn't set eyes on him for about five years until we ran into each other this morning.'

'He was in Singapore at one time, I understand. Is that where you met him?'

'Among other places. Our paths have crossed more than once. Why are you so interested? He's not on your wanted list, by any chance?'

'No, nothing like that. He's living down in my part of the world just now and I was introduced to him by a mutual friend. Singapore came up in the conversation at one point, in connection with another local resident, who's just met a sticky end, curiously enough. I wouldn't have expected you to have much in common with Gillford, though. Rather a strait-laced sort of man, I'd have thought.'

'Yes, I noticed that when I was talking to him just now, but he used to have his lighter side, too. Quite a lad in his time, I gather. Probably taken on local colour now, got himself a new persona to go with the new surroundings.'

'Which is not something that has happened to you?'

'I'd hate to think so. In any case, it wouldn't work with me for more than a week. I wouldn't have the stamina for it. Probably comes naturally to Gillford, he was always a bit of a dark horse.'

'His wife seems a straightforward enough character.'

'Janet? Oh yes, nice woman. A bit too good to be true, I sometimes used to think, but that may have been an act too.'

'She struck me as the sort who saw as much as it suited her to see, no less and no more; but then I've only met her once. Talking of bygone days, though, did you ever come across a character called Waddington on your travels?'

'Jim Waddington?'

'Well, yes, that would be the one.'

'Mainly by reputation, although I did

meet him in a casual sort of way on one or two occasions. He was another mystery, in his way. Someone told me he'd ended up getting killed in a car crash, but I don't know how true that was either. Got time for a liqueur before we move on?'

'Better not, thanks all the same. My henchman will be turning up to collect me in a moment and we mustn't set a bad example by parking illegally for longer than we can help.'

He would have been happy to have prolonged the conversation, with or without a liqueur, for at least a few more minutes but felt it would be imprudent to do so. Having denied any professional interest, further probing would inevitably arouse suspicion. Guy should now be filed away as a possible source of information, if and when it was needed.

'Any luck with the Wickers?' Tubby asked, as they waited for the lights to change at the top of St James's Street.

'I suppose it could be described as a small step forward,' Frank replied. 'I called at the Kensington agency, as you suggested, and spoke to the head lady. She told me they had since been taken on by an elderly widow in Buckinghamshire, a Mrs Stafford, while her permanent staff take their annual leave in their Spanish homeland. I've got the address, but that was about all she was willing to part with. I suggested to her that they changed jobs rather frequently, but she was not to be drawn on that. Realising, no doubt, that I might be better informed than I had let on, she said that the majority of her clients only wanted such services for short periods, the present case being an example and it was quite commonplace for people on her books to shuttle around between half a dozen jobs in as many months.'

'And I see no reason to disbelieve her. She'd soon be out of business if she made a practice of hiring out staff who couldn't hold down a job for more than three weeks. Still, you'd better go down and call on the Buckinghamshire lady tomorrow and get a closer look. Oh, here already, are we? Very high class, isn't it? Residents' parking space, too, so we'll be able to stay within the law this time.'

'Aged twenty-three, but looks younger, very attractive and probably tough, with it,' had been Frank's verdict. To less experienced observers, tough might not have been the epithet which sprang to mind, for there was no hint of it in her appearance or manner, frailty, in fact, being the name of Mrs Waddington. She was very small, not above five feet and so thin as to look almost emaciated. She was also wearing heavily rimmed glasses, which somehow contributed to the fragile look.

'Oh . . . hello . . . do come in, won't you?' she said, having opened the door to them herself.

When they had done so, she remained on her feet, saying hesitantly, 'I don't know what you think, but it seems rather early for tea. Perhaps you'd rather have coffee? It will only take a minute.'

'Thank you, if it's really no trouble, coffee would be very nice,' Tubby said, 'but you must let my Sergeant bring it in for you,' and when they had gone, fairly bounced out of his chair again and, secure in the knowledge that Frank could be depended upon to stretch a minute into five or six, started on a tour of inspection. He had no expectation of guilty revelations, but was not one to pass up an opportunity to glean a few insights, however superficial, into the tastes and habits of his hostess.

The first move was to verify that the three

paintings were indeed original works by Hockney, Paul Nash and Passmore. Next to come under review was the Regency sofa table, which, with the window above it, made the fourth wall. There was a bowl of mixed flowers, looking as though they had been delivered from the florist that morning, occupying the central position, a pile of books and magazines in front of it and some framed photographs dotted around in the remaining space. The largest of these had two or three snapshots tucked in between the glass and the frame, one of which aroused his curiosity enough for him to take it out for a closer look. It showed him a group of half a dozen people, all but one of whom, standing a little apart from the rest, wore riding clothes. Most of the faces were obscured by the peaked riding hats, but Sam Waddington and his then bride-to-be were both hatless and clearly identifiable in the centre of the group. He was back in his chair, turning the pages of one of the magazines and with the snapshot safely tucked away in his inside pocket by the time the other two returned. Mrs Waddington led the way, holding the door open for Frank, who carried a tray set out with an electric coffee pot, some unexpectedly cosy-looking cups and saucers and a plate of assorted biscuits.

'I hope you won't mind my asking this,' he said, 'I'm afraid we do have to plague people with what must seem rather absurd questions in our job, but would I be right in assuming that this is a furnished flat which your husband had rented for the two of you after your marriage?'

'Oh, no,' she replied with a sad little smile, 'quite wrong, I'm afraid. I don't think I could bear to go on living here, if that were so. No, this is my own flat, which I moved into two years ago, when my first marriage broke up and these are all my own things.'

'I see. And this has been your home ever since?'

'Most of the time. I travel quite a lot. In fact, some very dear friends in California are insisting on my spending a few months with them as soon as . . . things get sorted out a bit.'

'So no job or regular occupation of any kind?'

'Well, no, it would be such a tie, wouldn't it? And, to be perfectly honest, I don't really need to earn my own living. All the same, I don't want you to take me for a complete parasite. I help out quite a bit for an old friend who owns an antique shop.'

'But not on a regular basis?'

'No, it's usually when he has to be out of London for a sale, or something, but I also try and put in two or three mornings a week between May and July, which is the peak period for the tourists. I don't get any salary, in case that's your next question, just commission on anything I sell. And that's only because my friend insists on it. As I say, I don't need the money and I ought to be paying him, really. I enjoy the work and it brings me into contact with all sorts of weird and amazing people. Also old furniture happens to be one of the few subjects I do know a bit about.'

'That I can tell,' Tubby said, casting an admiring eye round the room and adding by way of afterthought, 'And this shop where you help out is in London, you said?'

This time there was more of genuine amusement than sadness in her smile and she said, 'Yes, indeed, right in the centre of London. Only just round the corner from here, in fact, which makes it so convenient for both of us. The name is Marriner, in case you're interested; Paul Marriner in

South Audley Street. About half way down on the right, going towards Piccadilly.'

'Well, thank you, Mrs Waddington, you've been exceptionally kind and patient. I expect you've been wondering what the purpose of all these questions is, but it's really just a matter of trying to fill in some of the background detail immediately prior to the fire. However, we mustn't take up any more of your time now. I gather you haven't anything relevant to add, which might help us to discover who committed this dreadful crime, otherwise you would have said so. It was hardly to be expected, but, since the case looks like dragging on for some time, I'm afraid I may have to ask your permission to call again. In the meantime, if something should occur to you which might help us, please do let me know at once. How about taking that tray out to the kitchen before we leave, Frank?'

'Oh, please don't bother,' she began, but Frank was already gathering it up.

'Exceptionally patient,' Tubby repeated when they were alone, 'and restrained too. I noticed you hadn't produced a single question of your own.'

'I? Ask you questions? Whatever would I want to do that for?'

'Oh, I don't know. You might have shown some curiosity about how the case was progressing, whether we were any nearer to finding out what happened that night, all that kind of thing. That would have been the reaction of a good many people.'

'Would it? Then I consider they would have been wasting their time. It's not that I'm indifferent, I assure you. I think of practically nothing else from the moment I wake up in the morning, but it never crossed my mind that you would tell me anything I didn't already know, or couldn't guess, however much I might question you. Besides,' she added in a different tone and turning her head aside, 'knowing more about it wouldn't help much, would it? Nothing in the world is going to bring Sam back or let me forget the horrible way he died.'

She took a deep breath, as of one fighting back the tears, removed her glasses, which she laid on the table beside her and pressed her index fingers against the inner corners of her eyes.

'I'm sorry, Mrs Waddington. I didn't mean to upset you.'

'You haven't,' she replied briskly. 'I'm

perfectly all right now,' and was making a move to pick up her glasses again when Frank came back.

'There's a strange woman in your kitchen,' he told her. 'She was using the telephone, but she rang off when I went in. I suppose it's all right? She said her name was Barbara.'

Until that moment Tubby, who had had Mrs Waddington under almost continuous observation, had felt sure that her every word and gesture had conformed to the image which she had set out to present to them. He did not believe that this necessarily implied that she was lying, or concealing anything of importance, more likely that she was someone who habitually played her cards warily and was constantly on her guard. However, just for a second, when Frank made his announcement the mask slipped and she stared up at him with an expression of anger, or fear, or possibly a combination of the two. It passed, however, and a moment later the smile was back in place.

'Oh, that's all right,' she assured them. 'There's nothing strange about Bar and the gruff manner is only a form of shyness. She's an old friend who's very kindly volunteered to come and take care of me for a few days and fend off unwelcome telephone calls.'

'Yes, I thought it must be something like that. She seemed a bit edgy, that's all. Still, I expect it was just the shock of seeing a strange man in your kitchen. I tried to explain that, if I was a real burglar, I most likely wouldn't have been invited to stay for coffee and I think she took the point in the end. Hope so, anyway.'

'I hope so too. We wouldn't want her ringing up the police to report it, would we? But no need to worry. Bar's very sweet really.'

'And we must take our leave,' Tubby said. 'We've caused quite enough havoc for one afternoon. Goodbye, Mrs Waddington and thank you again.'

She insisted on escorting them to the lift and while they were waiting for it to come up Frank remembered that he had left his briefcase behind and went back to retrieve it.

'What was all that about?' Tubby asked him, as they alighted on the ground floor.

'Just a dodge to get a closer look at those specs of hers.'

'And?'

'As I suspected. Pure, unadulterated, un-treated glass. Expensive rims too. Why would anyone go to all that trouble and expense for something so useless?'

'Perhaps it's a way of distancing herself from what's going on, or to add that dash of mystery . . . enigma.'

'I don't know why she'd bother. She has enough going for her already, I'd have thought.'

'Then, try this. She thinks women who wear glasses look truthful, serious and, above all, respectable.'

'She'd have to be out of her mind. Who wants respectability, I'd like to know?'

Tubby was thinking that pretty women certainly brought out the frisky side in Frank and that a timely reminder might now be in order. 'You had better ask your wife,' he said. 'She'll be able to explain it to you precisely.'

So, all things considered, not a wasted day and the best was yet to come. That evening after dinner and with a glass of vintage port within reach of his left hand, he succeeded in breaking the code and deciphering the note which had been left in the pocket of Sam Waddington's jacket. Admittedly, the significance remained obscure, but at least the text was clear and simple. It ran as follows: 'What's in a name? Not much for most of us, perhaps, but some are different. For some it's money, position and power and no good will come to the man who steals it from another.'

——Fourteen——————

'I was talking to a fellow member of your club yesterday,' Janet said. 'It turns out that he's a policeman, so perhaps you should watch your step.'

Unaccustomed to such badinage, Geoffrey climbed on to the highest horse in his stable. 'Who is this personage, how did you come to be talking to him and what gave you the impression that he is a member of my club?'

'You know that I went over to have lunch with Avril yesterday because she'd heard of a house which is coming on the market quite soon and might do for us? She'd invited us both, but I told her that you had to be in London all day.'

'Yes, yes, I do recall some talk of it.'

'She said that wouldn't matter because we

shouldn't be able to go inside, anyway. It was just to get an idea of the size and situation and so on and I could do that equally well on my own.'

'And so you decided to go. I do wish you'd come to the point and stop telling me things that I already know.'

'I decided to go because, although we now know we can stay here for another six months if we want to, so there's no desperate hurry, I thought it might be fun to spend a little time on my own with Avril.'

'Only you weren't on your own, it appears.'

'For most of the time, we were. This man was there when I arrived, but he didn't stay for lunch.'

'Only long enough to tell you that he was a member of my club?'

'Well, naturally, he didn't throw it out just like that. The three of us were talking of this and that and then he mentioned some book he'd been reading which he thought might interest you. I'd met him before, you see, we both had. He was at the lunch party Avril laid on for us at Easter, the fat one they all called Tubby.'

'Oh yes, I remember. So he's also a member of the constabulary, is he? Not on a very high level, if I'm any judge.'

'Why do you say that?' she asked, gaining time.

'Because I had a brief talk with him after lunch. He was pleasant enough, but he didn't seem to be particularly well informed on various subjects I tried him out on, including, ironically enough, the critical state of law and order in this country. Gave the impression of being half asleep, as a matter of fact, which is perhaps not surprising, in view of all the wine he managed to put away at lunch.'

Janet had thought of a tactful reply by this time and she said, 'Well, the thing is, Geoffrey, after he'd gone, Avril told me that he's the Chief Superintendent for all the branches, or whatever they call them, in this part of Sussex. But I daresay you're right. That's probably a sort of sinecure job which they hand out to people as a reward for long service. I expect there are all sorts of Inspectors and Sergeants buzzing about, doing all the real work and he's just a figurehead.'

Even Geoffrey couldn't quite accept this, but he found a compromise by saying, 'And, of course, in a well-heeled society, like we have down here, with nothing more serious to deal with than the occasional stolen car and routine burglary . . .' then, recollecting just in time a recent case of murder and arson, drove the ball rapidly into the adversary's court by adding, 'However, as usual, we seem to have strayed from the point. As to which, I think you must be mistaken, unless he's a very new member, for I certainly don't remember seeing him at the club in all the years I've been using it.'

'Well, I wouldn't know about that, of course, but he sounded very positive about having seen you there yesterday morning.'

'Ha!' Geoffrey said, the light of triumph gleaming from his eye. 'Splendid powers of deduction! As it happened, I didn't set foot in the Army and Overseas yesterday morning, but at twelve-fifteen precisely I had an appointment to meet a chap I'd been introduced to a few weeks ago who's quite a power in the publishing world and who may be willing to act as my agent. He'd suggested our having a talk about it at the Sackville, of which he happens to be a member, as presumably is your Mr Wiseman.'

'He's not my Mr Wiseman and I don't know why you have to treat my every casual remark as though I were a witness in court and it was your job to tear everything I say to pieces and make be look like a fool or a liar.'

'Oh, do forgive me. I hadn't realised it was such a sensitive subject. In future, I must be more careful of my words.'

In fact, it was one of those rare occasions when he had hit the nail squarely on the head, for it was not simply his sneering manner which for once had caused her to lose control. Nor was it just the repetition of this insulting pretence that the business which so often took him to London for the night was connected with his autobiography which, to her certain knowledge, consisted of less than a hundred pages of longhand and fell somewhat short in accuracy within the normal parameters of memoir writing. There was more to it than that, although what it was appeared to her in the form of shadow, rather than substance. It continued to hover over her for the rest of that day, and it was not until she woke from a bad dream during the night and recalled the scrap of paper which had fallen from the brochure that she realised why this conversation with Geoffrey had had such a disturbing effect on her.

Fifteen

'Anything of interest on the Wickers?' Tubby asked the next morning.

'So-so,' Frank replied, obeying the sign language command to seat himself on the other side of the desk. 'Broad End has become an outer suburb of High Wycombe. Still a few remnants left of the original village, but it's got a couple of small factories now and the main street is crammed with building societies and bathroom fittings. Overton House, where the Wickers are employed, is three-quarters of a mile further on towards Oxford and still relatively isolated. I'm only telling you this because it does have a slight bearing on what follows.'

'Very well, continue in your own fashion.'

'Mrs Stafford answered the door herself. Very spry, for one of her advanced age and sharp as a needle. That has a bearing too.'

Tubby nodded and Frank went on, 'Having established that the Wickers were still in her employ, I went through the routine about hoping I hadn't picked an inconvenient time to call and that she would have no objection to my talking to them for a few minutes. I explained that neither of them was under any kind of suspicion and that, although my enquiries were connected with a fire which had broken out in the house where they had recently been employed, there was obviously nothing they could tell me about that. However, since the building had been razed to the ground, we were trying to find out something about the household routine during the weeks preceding it, and so on and so on.'

'And had she any objection?'

'None whatever. Thoroughly entered into the spirit of the thing and was most co-operative. She'd heard all about the fire from the Wickers, who'd read the news-paper reports and she'd be glad to take me to the kitchen and introduce me to Mrs Wicker.'

'Any surprises there?'

'There was one, as it happens, or rather, on the way there. It's one of those rambling, old-fashioned houses, with rooms opening off a long corridor and must take a hell of a lot of upkeep, but it all looked in re-markably good trim. When I remarked on this to Mrs Stafford she said that her regular Spanish couple were absolute paragons in that way and the Wickers were cut from the same cloth. She couldn't speak too highly of them.'

'Which doesn't quite tally with the reputation they acquired for themselves at Uppfield.'

'Or had thrust upon them, perhaps? Anyway I suggested to the old lady that she must be exceptionally lucky, since I'd been told that with most married couples in this line of business one half of the partnership was apt to be first-rate and the other virtually useless. She said she'd heard so too, but it certainly didn't apply to the Wickers. Anyway, we'd got as far as the kitchen by this time, so she took me in and introduced me and left us to it.'

'And what sort of a welcome did you get from Mrs Wicker?'

'Quite unruffled. She's not easily thrown, I should imagine. Very much in control and a trifle bitten up, but perfectly civil and responsive, without ever volunteering anything of her own. Early fifties at a guess, and no question about her talents, judging by the fish soufflé she was knocking up for her lady's dinner. I asked her one or two questions about the domestic routine at Uppfield, which I either didn't need to know or knew already and when we'd been through that pantomime I suggested that it must have been a nasty shock to hear about the fire, to which she replied that, in a way, it was and, then again, she wasn't all that surprised.'

'In which way wasn't she?'

'It was a reference to her late employer's habit of smoking like a chimney and letting the ash fall where it listeth. If you remember, Mrs Waddington made much the same comment.'

'Yes, she did and not the only one to have harped on that theme. Alice Wilkes was full of complaints about it. Still, as we've agreed, however careless he may have been in that respect, they can hardly expect us to believe that he would have dropped a lighted cigarette on to a pile of rags which had been doused in paraffin. Was that all you got from Mrs Wicker?'

'Yes, I decided to leave it there. I had to keep up the pretence that I was only interested in the day-to-day running of Uppfield, but her husband was my prime target and I was hoping for better things from him.'

'Any luck?'

'She told me that I'd be likely to find him in or near the greenhouse, as he was very busy just now planting out the summer annuals. I thought that sounded like a suitable programme for one of his reputation and that in all probability I'd find him tucked away in the greenhouse, with his head in the racing news and a bottle of beer keeping cool in a flower pot, but I was wrong. One or two of the beds I passed on my way down had recently been planted out and when I tracked him down he was working away, good as gold, potting up some geranium cuttings. When I'd been through the usual routine, I said it had been reported to us that he'd been in the vicinity of Uppfield on Easter Sunday and, if true, perhaps he'd care to tell me for what purpose.'

'Which he categorically denied, no doubt?'

'With knobs on. The story was that he'd had the weekend off and, despite not having any fond memories of Uppfield, they'd become attached to Bexhill during their stay and that was where they had planned to spend it. No, they hadn't driven straight there and back, it being a longish drive. They'd stopped for a snack at a pub about twenty miles short of it. So it must have been someone from around Redlye that had seen them there. Not all that surprising if they had, it being a Bank Holiday and no reason why he or his wife should have noticed them, what with all that crush and crowd of people and the trouble they'd had trying to find somewhere to sit down to eat their lunch. When I told him that our information claimed to have seen him much closer to Uppfield than that, actually in the grounds, in fact, he was quite unabashed. There were lots of people around Uppfield, one family in particular, who got up to no end of tricks when Mr Waddington was away and it wouldn't be the first time they'd shoved the blame on him or his wife. Seeing him in that pub, or maybe just their car outside, would have given them just the chance they needed to try it on again.'

'So he absolutely denied having been at Uppfield himself?'

'Absolutely and there didn't seem much to be gained by pressing the point. Every word he said could have been true and I was on rather shaky ground, with only Miss Kershaw's evidence to go on.'

'Oh well, another wasted journey, by the sound of it. Still, it had to be done.'

'There was just one point, right at the end, which might be worth considering,'

Frank said hesitantly. 'A sort of postscript, you might say.'

'And, knowing your incurable habit of keeping the *bonne bouche* for the postscript, you had better tell me about it.'

'It was when I took my leave of Mrs Stafford. She asked me if my journey had been worthwhile and I said that only insofar as it had served to confirm one or two points which had been in doubt, or some such rigmarole, and I added that they appeared to be an excellent pair, and no doubt she considered herself to be fortunate to have them in these hard times. She said, "Yes, indeed," and if it were in her power she would make it a regular annual arrangement. "So why not?" I asked her, and then it turns out that the Wickers are planning to retire and this will be their swan song in this kind of life. They've had a windfall in the form of a house in Scarborough, left to Mrs Wicker by an aunt and, as soon as they've sold it, they plan to move to the West Country and set up in business on their own.'

'What kind of business?'

'Small restaurant, private hotel, something in the catering line and, in her view, they'd be bound to make a success of it, whatever it was. Thinking it over on the way home, it struck me that there was something out of place about it. For one thing, the agency woman hadn't said a word about it and I can't help feeling from the way she spoke of them that it will come as news to her. And, although Mrs Wicker fits in fairly well with the description we've had from people here who knew her, Wicker has so little resemblance to everything we've heard about him that I began to wonder . . .'

'Whether she had switched husbands somewhere along the line?'

'Not so much that as whether the new prosperity and the new persona might be due not to a Scarborough windfall, but to another kind of lucky investment.'

'Such as a small venture into blackmail, for instance?'

'Oh, you agree that might account for it?' Frank asked with evident relief.

'The thought had flashed into my mind, as it happens.'

'And it would also account for Miss Kershaw having seen him drive up from the house and then go into the Lodge that morning. If he and his wife had turned up something promising in the way of blackmail material during their stay at Uppfield, what better day to come back and collect the hard evidence than a Bank Holiday, when they knew the coast would be clear?'

'It's a nice theory, I agree, and it would be good news to find that my old friend, Miss Kershaw, isn't losing her marbles, but the fact is that we have small hope of ever finding out whether it's the right one. If Waddington was paying them hush money, there'd be a fat chance of tracing it now and there certainly won't be any more payments in the future. I do wonder, though if the Wickers are responsible for nothing more sinister than making an anonymous phone call about what they presumed to be a murder at Uppfield. If Miss Kershaw had not been so vague about the time she saw them I'd pin that one on them with no hesitation at all. As it is, I fear we must consign that call to the ever-growing list of unsolved mysteries which surround the doings at Uppfield Court.'

Sixteen

Miranda's faith in the sagacity of her old friend remained unshaken by the disclosure which finally cleared up the mystery of Rupert's wayward behaviour, although it brought numerous other problems in its wake.

Far from his irritability and moodiness indicating, as he explained to her, that he was any less in love, it was the very fear of losing her which had caused them. The trouble was that his solution to the problem only led to a reversal of their roles. What it amounted to was that she had now to choose between giving him up for ever, or marrying him and spending the rest of her life in Canada and, if that wasn't a prospect to send any normal person into fits of moodiness and irritability, she would have liked someone to tell her what was.

Not that this had been her first reaction to the news. The immediate one had been to declare that she would follow him to the ends of the earth, if need be. Whereupon he had leant forward over the secluded little table in the quiet little restaurant, gathered up both her hands in his and implanted a kiss on each, a gesture which, unaccountably, she found rather affected and embarrassing. It was not the first time he had performed this ritual, only first time she had found it affected and embarrassing and, reverting to a more down-to-earth tone, she asked, 'But why does it have to be Canada?'

'It doesn't have to be,' he replied, 'but at this point in my life it does seem to have the most to offer as the land of promise. I have to break out on my own and get right away somewhere, you see. Oh, not from you, my love, you know that by now, or should do. In fact, I'd have been ready to scrub the idea if you'd given it the thumbs down. I really mean that, even though I know in my heart I'd feel restless and frustrated for the rest of my life if I had to buckle down and carry on here in the same old routine. You couldn't exactly call that a very good augury for married bliss, could you?'

'I suppose not, but why would you feel restless and frustrated? It wouldn't, by any chance, have something to do with this scheme for turning the countryside into one vast new town and leisure centre?'

'Not especially, no, although it certainly isn't designed to improve my father's outlook on life. He's becoming practically paranoic on the subject.'

'And it's your father you're really trying to escape from, isn't it? Well, I can sympathise, up to a point. I have a bit of trouble with my own, from time to time, as you know, but I never saw myself emigrating to Canada on that account.'

'Oh, for God's sake, Miranda, we're talking about two entirely different situations, can't you see that? Oh, I'm sorry, darling, I didn't mean to fly at you, but do try and look at it from my point of view.'

'Believe me, I am trying.'

'Well, all right then, you say you don't always see eye to eye with your father and I believe you, but it doesn't affect your life very much, does it? There you are, at the age of eighteen, taking off to live on your own in London and become a ballet dancer, for a start.'

As it happened, Miranda had already begun to think of that very thing and it occurred to her that internationally respected ballet companies might be rather thin on the ground in Canada and the opportunities for pursuing her career somewhat restricted. However, she felt reluctant to point this out now, having started on such a noble, self-sacrificing note and, in any case, it was not the moment because Rupert was now well away on his own deprivations and disappointments.

'While, as for me,' he was saying, 'I was packed off to some dim boarding school. My mother became ill just about that time and my father thought it would make things easier for her if she didn't have me to look after. When I finished there she was dead and my father was engrossed in his feud with Waddington and insisting that I chuck my place at Cambridge and go to agricultural college to be able to take over from him when he kicked the bucket.'

Miranda attempted a few soothing noises, but Rupert was not in the mood to be soothed.

'Imagine, I was expected to spend every weekend at home. Back for supper on Friday evening on the dot and not allowed to leave till dawn on Monday, come hell or high water. And what do you suppose we talked about during those long and boring weekends? The Waddington case and rotten bloody farming, that's what! Oh, don't look at me like that, Miranda darling. I know it sounds feeble, but I'd been brainwashed, you see. All my life, since I was six years old, it had been going on. First, there was the moral blackmail of my mother's illness and then after she died it was his turn. There he was, poor old sod, missing her obsessively, every minute of the day, with only myself to bring a ray of light into his cheerless life and the knowledge that he was keeping the farm going, so as to hand it over to me in good trim when the time came, to provide him with the incentive to go on living at all. How would you have felt?'

'Well, no, it can't have been much fun for you, I realise that,' Miranda admitted, 'but, all the same, I still don't see . . .'

'No, it wasn't,' he said, too engrossed in his own grievances to allow her to finish, 'and the real, decisive crunch came about six months ago.'

'When you got engaged to Annie?'

'Exactly. I haven't dragged her into it before because I wouldn't want you to get any fatuous idea that I had regrets, or anything. In fact, sitting across the table from you now, the only emotion I feel for her is a great big burst of gratitude for having been the one to break it off.'

'All the same, you have dragged her in, so what were you going to say about her?'

'Well, you see, angel, the real truth, and one realises it now, is that the scales have fallen. She was only the means to an end and the end, believe it or not, was marriage. I had got to the point of seeing it as the only way to escape from the stultifying cage that had been built round me and I was a sitting duck for any presentable female who showed an interest. And then, do you know what happened? Well, of course you do. I'd no sooner broken the news to my father, hardly got the words out about not losing a son, but gaining a daughter, than he'd hit on a new way to chain me up for life. The next thing I knew was that he'd gone out and bought, actually bought without consulting me, a house for us just down the road from his own. Could you beat it?'

'Not really, no. With all his faults, I can't see my Dad going to those lengths,' Miranda said comfortingly, though for the life of her she couldn't see why this had been such an awful crime. In these days of expensive housing many young couples would have happily sacrificed the independence of their heavy mortgages for such a start to their married life.

'Of course he wouldn't. There can't be another father alive who would behave like that and imagine he could get away with it. He's absolutely crazy and obsessed and all I've done by letting him get away with it is to tip him right over the edge. Anyway, as soon as I was faced with that little package deal I realised the error of my ways and that something drastic had to be done to straighten things out. Thank God Annie made it so easy for me. The house has now been disposed of for the time being, but it's only a temporary reprieve, you can bet your life on that. As soon as I tell him about you and me he'll turf the tenants out, or else rush off and buy us some other little cosy nook and I'm just not having it.'

Miranda had been under the clearly erroneous impression that Mr James Crossman had already been informed of his son's impending happiness with his new bride-to-be. The fact that this was not the case added fuel to the smouldering worries concerning her engagement. 'And you see Canada as the only solution?' she asked, unable to eradicate totally the concern from her voice.

'I don't say the only one, but it looks like a good option to me. It would be absolutely useless to fool ourselves that we could stay anywhere around here, or in fact anywhere at all in this country. If we fetched up in Scotland or Land's End he'd be perfectly capable of selling the farm and coming to live on our doorstep.'

'Well, I don't know, Rupert. I mean, it's quite a big step, isn't it? It's going to take a bit of adjusting to. Had you any particular part of Canada in mind?'

'I thought, on the whole, that British Columbia might be our best bet.'

'Because it's the furthest away from your father?'

'Well, it has that in its favour, admittedly, but I was thinking of the climate. Also the kind of farming they go in for there is more what I'm used to. But listen, love, you don't have to adjust all in one leap, you know. Neither of us does. What I thought was that I'd nip over there on my own for three or four weeks and spy out the land, maybe put a few irons in the fire and then come back and report on the situation. Then, if you agree, we could get married here in the conventional style and tell everyone we're going to spend our honeymoon in Canada. That way, you'll be able to see the farm without committing yourself in advance. If you like the idea of living there, we can go ahead with our plans. If not, well nothing lost, we just come back here and mark time till something else turns up to get us off the hook.'

'You've certainly got it all worked out, haven't you?' Miranda said, wondering in a glum sort of way what the ballet scene consisted of in Vancouver.

'Well, yes, I suppose you could say that. It's been engaging my mind for quite a while now, but there's one thing we've got to get straight, Miranda. Everything depends on you. If, after all, you find you couldn't be happy out there, we scrap the whole idea. In any case, I don't expect you to answer yes or no straight off. Just think about it for a bit and then let me know if you're game to have a go. Will you do that?'

'Okay,' Miranda said, 'I'll think about it.'

Seventeen

'Do you consider heredity to be a vital factor?' Miranda asked her father at breakfast the following morning.

'I suppose it must be, but I have never given much thought to the subject,' he replied. 'There are moments when you bear a startling resemblance to your mother, as she looked at about your age, but I see no evidence that you have inherited any other characteristics from either of us, if that's what's bothering you.'

'It isn't. I was thinking about other people's heredity.'

'Well, yes, I can see that might be more of a worry,' he said, watching her closely as she went through the performance of dissecting an apple. 'Anyone in particular?'

'Not especially, no.'

So now Billy, too, had something to think about.

Twenty minutes later, when he had stopped doing so and transferred his attention to the main story in the *West Sussex Gazette*, Tubby walked in.

'Miranda told me where to find you,' he explained. 'I am sorry to call so early, but if I'd left it any later, you'd probably have been out in your studio and beyond the reach of human contact.'

'Times have changed,' Billy told him, pouring coffee for them both. 'Only temporarily, I trust, but in the present stalemate I can neither concentrate on work no longer in hand, nor force myself to look about for something to take its place.'

'In the meantime, I gather you've been diverting your mind from these problems by reading about the inquest?'

'Yes, and I see that arson is the name of the crime.'

'Inevitable, wouldn't you say?'

'I suppose so. There doesn't seem to be any hint of his having set fire to the place himself?'

'No. Obviously, the insurance people had

been hoping for that, but there isn't a shred of evidence to support it. Even the fact that he had recently increased the cover didn't help them, since it's quite a normal thing for a newly married man to have done. The main obstacle, of course, was that the idea of someone setting fire to his own house in order to claim the insurance and then going upstairs to bed was too preposterous to be taken seriously. So where does it leave you?'

'Exactly where I was before. Assuming the new owner is ready to go along with it, an appeal will be lodged against the Council's veto, but it's likely to be many moons before we get to the court hearing. Not so for you, I imagine? For your lot, I daresay, the action is only just beginning?'

'That's partly true, although we haven't exactly been twiddling our thumbs, which is partly why I am here now.'

'Yes, I wondered when we were coming to that.'

'I'd like you to take a look at this snapshot,' Tubby said, placing it on top of the newspaper. 'You may be able to remember when it was taken and whether you recognise any of the people, apart from yourself and Waddington, of course.'

'And I was not there by intention,' Billy

said, holding the photograph within an inch of his nose. 'I'd brought some papers for Waddington to take back to London with him. It was a Sunday and they'd all been out riding, as you can see; I hadn't realised there was a photography session in progress until I stepped into the middle of it. The other three were all youngish people, who'd come down for the weekend. It was some time last September or October, to the best of my recollection.'

'Had you seen any of them before?'

'I may have. He often brought an assortment down for weekends, or for the day on Sunday. I think the tall boy was American, but I couldn't be sure. I might be mixing him up with someone else.'

'How about the two young women?'

'Well, you can't see much of their faces, can you? But I think I've seen the little blonde girl before; more than once in fact.'

'Does the name Susannah mean anything to you?'

'Not that I recall. What's her surname?'

'It's changed since then. She's now Mrs Sam Waddington.'

'Oh, is that the one? Well, no great surprise, really. She's very attractive and you can see from his expression here how his mind was working. Still, if you know so much, why do you need my help?'

'Just filling in the background, I suppose is what it amounts to. Trying to reconstruct events during the months before his death and unfortunately there's not a lot to go on. Several people have referred to these friends from London, who used to come down at weekends, but since the local community was kept firmly at bay and the domestic staff were more or less on a piece-work basis, no one seems to know much about them, except that they tended to be quite young. How about the photographer? You must have got a good view of him or her, since you are looking straight at the camera in this one.'

'I can't say that I remember much about it. It was a man, that much I do remember, and I suppose he was young too.'

'You suppose?'

'He would probably have made a deeper impression on me if he hadn't been.'

'And that's absolutely all you can remember?'

Billy took his glasses off and rubbed his eyes, as though they were hurting him. Then he said, 'The curious thing is, you know, that the more I try to picture it, the clearer the impression becomes that there was something out of place about him, and I mean literally out of place, which I must have noticed at the time in a sub-conscious kind of way, and then forgotten. It wasn't that he was older than the rest of them, or anything obvious and simple like that, and the harder I try to pin it down the faster it slips away.'

'Perhaps you had seen him somewhere before, in different surroundings?'

'It could have been that, I suppose. I honestly can't tell you.'

'Well, don't trouble yourself any more with it just now. It may not have any importance, and if it really did sink into your sub-conscious it could easily bob up to the surface again, when you least expect it.'

'I certainly hope you're right. If not, it's going to create havoc with my concentration for the foreseeable future.'

'And if you should manage to catch hold of it,' Tubby said, getting to his feet in his usual slow and ponderous fashion, 'do try and cling on and let me be the first to know.'

'I'll do that,' Billy assured him and, after a few minutes of solitary eye rubbing, shook his head in disgust and went back to the lead story in the *Gazette*.

It was only after he had moved on from that and was half way down the column headed 'Broken Romance leads to Motor Cycle Tragedy' that a picture flashed into his mind, exactly as Tubby had foretold. However, he was able to persuade himself that it could well be a false one and, in any case, it was far too vague and insubstantial to be worth passing on as it stood. After pondering the question for several more minutes, he managed to convince himself that the sensible course would be to delay matters until he had found the right way to approach Miranda on the subject, preferably during his lunch break, but, failing that, not later than seven or so that evening, when they met again for dinner.

——Eighteen——

'Now, who might this be, do you suppose?' Janet said, having formed the habit of chatting to herself in a bracing, games mistressy sort of way whenever the Hoover was switched on. The top half of a dark blue saloon car was just visible above the newly clipped hedge and she went on pushing the machine over the same patch of carpet by the window, as she awaited developments.

The suspense was soon over, although only to be replaced by further self-interrogation, and after some slight hesitation she sped across the room, plunged into the library without knocking and closed the door behind her.

'Terribly sorry to interrupt you, Geoffrey,' she spluttered, quite out of breath. 'I know it's against the rules, but we have a visitor and it's a bit awkward.'

'I didn't hear the bell. Who is this visitor?'

'Well, that's the point. It's that friend of Avril's, the Superintendent. He's walking up the path. Was walking up the path,' she amended as the doorbell rang. 'I'll have to go and let him in. Do you mind very much if I bring him in here?'

'Why? What's wrong with the sitting room?'

'Everything. I'm in the middle of turning it out and there isn't a chair to sit on. Look, I must go.'

'Oh, very well, if you insist,' he said, 'but at least give me five minutes. It can throw me out for the whole morning to be cut off in mid-stream like this.'

This reaction was so unlike the poorly concealed relief with which he normally greeted some trivial interruption that the unease which had come over her when she first sighted Mr Wiseman standing by the gate had turned into a deep foreboding by the time she reached the front door.

Tubby's opening words did something to restore her poise, however, taking the form of apologies for intruding at such an early hour, without so much as a by your leave, followed by a harmless sounding explanation for having done so.

'I had to come out this way and, knowing I'd be passing your door, saw it as a good opportunity to bring you the book you thought might interest your husband. Is he at home, by any chance?'

'Yes, hard at work in the library at present, but just about to break off for some coffee, so do come in and join us. I know he'd like to thank you himself. Sorry about all this chaos,' she went on, stopping to pick up a tin of polish and some dusters from the floor, as part of her efforts to fill up her allotted five minutes, 'I've been having a grand turn-out, as you can see.'

'And I should be the one to apologise,' he said, as she paused outside the library door, as though intending to knock and then thinking better of it. 'One shouldn't really drop in on people without warning, but I'm afraid we get into bad habits in our job.'

She was not sure whether to take this as a joke or not, but the feeling of unease came creeping back and as soon as she had handed him over to Geoffrey she spent a few minutes on some morale raising attention to her hair and face, before getting to work on the coffee.

'Avril tells me you've got a book of your own in progress,' Tubby said, having brought out the one which had been his excuse for calling and which Frank Ross had managed to track down in a Brighton book shop. 'How's it going?'

'Slowly, I regret to say. Not being a professional author, I find some difficulty in collating all the material, getting it into the right order and keeping the right balance, if you can understand what I mean?'

'Yes, I think I can, particularly as I understand you have travelled to so many parts of the world and met such a variety of people in your time. Still, I suppose you have diaries to draw on, which you kept as you went along?'

'Unfortunately not. I regret it now, of

course, but one doesn't think of these things at the time.'

'And I daresay there weren't many opportunities for it. Quite apart from the demands of your work, you must have had to master a good many foreign tongues, moving around from one country to another, as you did?'

'I can't claim to have become fluent in any of them. It wasn't really required of me. One picked up a few basic words and phrases in the local lingo, enough to make oneself understood by the servants and so on; but my task was to introduce and promote our language and culture to the foreigners, so it would have been a waste of time to mug up on theirs.'

'Ah yes, stupid of me not to have realised that.'

'The only period when I did step out of line there, as they say now,' Geoffrey went on, expanding under the heady influence of this appreciative audience, 'was during my first posting, which was in Cyprus, while I was still a bachelor.'

'That must have been a delightful spot for a young man in those days?'

'Oh, indeed! I spent three very happy years there and they were great times, I can tell you, but of course I had no ties in those days.'

'And which of the languages did you take on? Turkish or Greek?'

'Oh, Greek. It was the obvious one. All the young intellectuals in those days were Greek-speaking and they were the type I wanted to attract to the kind of things the Council could provide. Besides, I'd done a certain amount of classical Greek at school, which gave me a start. Did you know, incidentally, that Cypriot Greek is closer to the ancient version than the one now spoken in Athens?'

'No, I didn't. How very interesting! Nevertheless, you found no difficulty in picking it up?'

'No, I had become reasonably fluent by the time I left, but I soon realised the folly of repeating the exercise. Greek, in any form, was no use to me at all in my next posting, which was in Africa and after that I spent eight years in Bangkok. Not much opportunity to practise it there.'

'Still, it brought its own rewards, no doubt. There is a saying that no effort, however useless it may seem, is ever wholly wasted,' Tubby suggested, this being one of his own precepts in discouraging periods.

'I remember when I was in my last year at school, I was no great classical scholar, but one or two of us fifth formers joined ourselves into a sort of secret society and we used the Greek alphabet as our means of communication. That's to say, the words were in English, but the script was Greek. I daresay it's a dodge that's been popular with every generation of schoolboys since time began, but we thought we'd invented something entirely new and we got a lot of fun out of it while it lasted.'

Annoyingly enough, Janet chose this moment to bring the coffee in and Geoffrey retreated into his shell and allowed her to prattle on uninterrupted about whether Tubby liked milk and sugar and what a pleasure it had been to meet Avril again, so little changed after all these years.

Tubby did not consider his mission to have been wasted, however, and by the time he returned to his office, had laid his plans for the next move, which was to contrive another meeting with Guy Kenton before the week was out.

When she had seen him off Janet went back to the library to collect the tray. Geoffrey was standing by the window with his back to her and when he turned round she saw a terrifying glint in his eye and he began to chortle aloud and rub his hands together like the Demon King in pantomime.

'So there you have it,' he said. 'Doesn't that prove my words?'

'I don't know, Geoffrey. What were your words?'

'When I was talking to that man at your friend Avril's party, we got on to the subject of the Greek islands and I happened to mention that I'd spent a few years in Cyprus in my early days with the Council. He seemed interested enough at the time, in his sleepy way, but just now, when the subject came up again, he seemed surprised to learn that I'd ever been there in my life. I ask you! So much for our gimlet-eyed Detective Chief Superintendent!'

The dismay which had begun to invade Janet forty minutes earlier, took a firmer grip than ever. In all the years of ministering to his needs and of training herself to interpret his every expression and inflexion of speech, this was the first time she had ever caught him putting on such a pitiful performance of whistling in the dark.

─Nineteen─

1

After all, Billy did not speak to Miranda on the subject uppermost in his mind either on that evening or the following day. This was partly due to his cowardice about being drawn into any kind of conflict, but Miranda's own demeanour did not encourage him to believe that he could do any good by stepping out of character on this occasion. She was not at all hostile, merely subdued and distrait and so unlike her usual cheerful, bossy self as to indicate that she was feeling just as uncertain as he was. Since, as he frequently reminded himself, Tubby had not laid any particular emphasis on the urgency of the matter, he preferred to let it slide for as long as possible.

On the third day, however, when she was getting ready to go back to London, she told him that she would not be down the following weekend and he had realised that the sliding times were over. Even he could not seriously contemplate shelving the whole business for another two, or, as it might turn out, three weeks and, grasping the nettle, he said, 'So you won't be seeing your fiancé either? Or does he mean to spend it in London too?'

'Not as far as I know.'

'And perhaps he wouldn't want to leave his father in the lurch?'

'I hope that doesn't indicate that you'll feel left in the lurch yourself?'

'No, certainly not, that is quite different. Has he broken the news to his father yet, by the way?'

'You mean about us getting married?'

'Yes, naturally. What else?'

'I don't know whether he has or not.'

'One way and another, Miranda, it strikes me that there's not an awful lot you do know about him.'

'Yes, there is. As much as I need to know, anyway.'

'I wonder if that's true. Are you aware, for instance, that he sometimes visited Uppfield Court when Waddington was alive?'

'He can't have. The Crossmans loathed Mr Waddington. Who on earth told you that?'

'Nobody needed to tell me. I saw him there myself.'

'I do believe you're serious,' she said, all

at once looking about twelve years old again. 'When did you see him?'

'On two occasions, both of them accidental. The second time was a couple of months ago. I'd called at Uppfield to deliver some sketches. The whole party had been out riding and the rest of them were lined up, having their photograph taken by your young man. I realised then, in a vague sort of way, that I'd seen him there once before, again when I dropped in more or less unexpectedly.'

'Why didn't you tell me this before?'

'Because until he came here to collect you and take you out to dinner I had no idea what he looked like, and the stupid thing is that even then I didn't make the connection. I recognised something familiar about him, but I attributed it to quite a different cause, such as having seen him at a point-to-point, or something of that sort. It wasn't until two or three days ago that the two pictures merged into one and I felt, well, I suppose I felt you ought to know about it, that's all.'

'Well, if it is,' she said, 'I'd better be getting a move on. Otherwise, I'll miss the lousy train.'

She looked so bewildered and defenceless

that Billy's heart sank and, to his great amazement, he heard himself say, 'No, don't go, Miranda. Why not take the day off, for once in your life? You're not looking at all well, haven't been looking well for days now and you'll only do yourself more damage if you go pounding up to London. In fact, I think it's time we both took a day off. We could go to Brighton if you like, and walk on the pier and have lobsters for lunch. Or we might find a film we want to see. How about it?'

'Okay,' she said, blinking her eyes rather rapidly. 'Why not? Tell you what, though, I'll go upstairs for a bit and change into my pier-strolling clothes and so on, but could you ring the school in about half an hour and explain? Ask to speak to Janine and tell her to make some grovelling excuses to Madame. Lay it on as thick as you can. You could say that I've been struck down by some mysterious and unidentifiable disease.'

And, if Janine could see you now, Billy thought to himself, she'd believe every word of it.

He could only be thankful for the fact that, so far as he could tell, she had not as yet jumped to any sinister conclusions, apart perhaps from the suspicion that the

227

love of her life was not the most open and above-board young man between here and the North Pole. Whereas, for his own part, he now no longer considered it would make a pennyworth of difference whether he passed on his little piece of information to Tubby Wiseman or not. Tubby probably knew all the answers already and Billy could only hope that the final unravelling of the happenings at Uppfield would not involve his daughter in anything more serious than a deeply bruised ego.

2

No aspect of human behaviour being too trivial to slip through the net, one who did spend the day in London was Tubby himself. It was an effort not wasted and he was rewarded, when he walked into the bar of the Sackville just before one o'clock by the sight of his quarry in conversation with one of the stewards.

'You lunching?' he asked, turning his attention to Tubby.

'That was the rough idea. How about you?'

'Might as well. I see they've got salmon

on the menu, which is usually quite tolerable.

'How's that case of yours coming along,' he asked when they were seated, 'the one that fellow Waddington got himself mixed up in?'

'Mixed up in is rather an understatement.'

'Yes, well, I take your point. I keep harking back to the idea that he's been dead for years and it distorts the picture. How's it going?'

'Not very rapidly. We shall get there in the end, I don't doubt, but it's a long haul.'

'Yes, I can see that. Fat lot of use crawling about with a magnifying glass over the scene of a crime like that. Whoever was responsible isn't likely to have left many clues strewn around where you can still find them.'

'Quite so, and that's not the only line of enquiry which is closed to us. In some ways, the victim poses as many questions as his assassin.'

'But at least you know who the victim was?'

'Oh yes, no problem there, but the trouble is that his personality seems to have gone up in smoke, along with everything else.

Nobody we've talked to seems to know much about him and until we fill in some of those gaps it's going to be uphill work finding someone with a powerful enough motive to want him out of the way.'

'Yes, he was always a bit of a loner, I suppose, looking back on it.'

'Anything else you recall when you look back?'

'Not a lot, that's the curious part of it. A detached sort of character, according to people who knew him well. Good humoured, good company, but just when he seemed to be settling down a bit, he'd be off again and on the move, never saying where or why he was going. Someone once put it around that he was a spy and he could have been, for all I know, but who for is hard to imagine. Not much help to you, am I?'

'No, but I get the impression that you, personally, found him likeable, in a detached kind of way?'

'Oh, he was all right. Not a brilliant conversationalist, but that cuts both ways, doesn't it? He was a good listener, which can be a much more endearing characteristic.'

'How about women?'

'Same story. He seemed to get on well

enough with them, but no serious attachments as far as one could tell, and no mention of a wife, past, present or in the offing.'

'How did he support himself, I wonder?'

'God knows. That was another mystery. According to his own story, he'd knocked around and done a good many jobs in his time; schoolmaster, courier, journalist, not to mention a spell in the merchant navy. Some of it must have been true, I suppose. He never gave the appearance of being particularly hard up.'

'Perhaps he was what they used to call a remittance man?'

'What's that, when it's at home?'

'Some black sheep ne'er do well getting a regular income from his family, on condition he remains out of the country and never darkens the ancestral doors.'

'Well, yes, that makes sense, I suppose. Clever of you to put your finger on it.'

'No, it's not. It's about the only explanation which ties in with what we know about him already. Still, it's been an interesting exercise, from several points of view and I'm grateful to you.'

'Not at all, my dear fellow. I've rather enjoyed this game of total recall. Surprising how it all starts flowing when you press the right button.'

'Good! So, if that's how you feel, let me try you out on a bit more. You say it's years since you saw the man, but can you pin it down a bit more closely?'

'Well, now, that does need a bit of thought, I admit. Let's see, now . . .'

He drifted off into silent concentration for a few minutes and then said, 'Something between eight and ten years. Can't get any closer than that.'

'So, if you were to pass him in the street this afternoon, do you think you'd still recognise him?'

'Unless he'd had the top half of his face blown away, I'm certain of it.'

'Because of the scar, you mean?'

'Yes. You ceased to notice it after the first few minutes, but if you saw him again after an interval it was the first thing that hit you.'

'And did he have it ever since you'd known him?'

'Yes. Yes, he did.'

'Well, thanks again. You've been most forbearing and some of what you've told me may turn out to be helpful.'

'I expect you know what you're doing,

but I should be interested to know what light it could possibly shed.'

'And so you shall, I promise you. If I'm right, you'll be hearing a lot about it, when the time comes.'

Twenty

1

'Who was that on the telephone?' Geoffrey asked, wandering in from the library soon after eleven on the following morning. It was a question he was beginning to ask ever more frequently, but this was the first time he had abandoned the daily stint at his desk in order to do so.

There was a time when Janet would have welcomed this development, seeing it as a triumph for her own diplomacy, but circumstances had changed since then and so, as she now began to realise, had she. Now that there was no longer any need to go galloping off to view every vacant house that came on the market, she was actually starting to regret the loss of her own isolation and independence during his working hours and the freedom they had provided to spend the morning as she chose, without the need to break off and give an account of her activities and their whys and wherefores.

'Only Avril,' she replied.

'Indeed? You seemed to have plenty to say to each other. About twenty minutes' worth, according to my reckoning.'

Janet sighed. 'Well, the thing is you see, Geoffrey, she was ringing me about that house she took me to see last week when you were in London. You remember?'

'Naturally, I do, since you were so set on going, I remember.'

'Yes, but that was before we knew we might be able to buy this one.'

'And it's still only a possibility. Nothing definite.'

'I realise that, Geoffrey, but it was obvious from what Mr Crossman told us yesterday that he definitely means to sell it. This business of his son taking a month off to go to Canada seems to have got it through to him at last that he'll never settle down here. I know it's not official yet, but I thought it only fair to let Avril know which way the wind was blowing before she goes to any more trouble on our behalf. And she agrees with me.'

'That she shouldn't go to any more trouble on our behalf?'

'No, of course not. She agrees that we should be mad not to snap this one up, if we get the chance. As she pointed out, every house has some disadvantages and, on the whole, the devil you know is preferable to the other kind. She also reminded me that, as sitting tenants, we'd probably get it at less than the going price, which is something I admit hadn't occurred to me.'

'Aren't you both taking rather a lot for granted?'

'No, I don't think so. You heard what Mr Crossman said yesterday about his son having set his mind on this Canadian venture?'

'Oh, certainly, but then I've heard a good many other things he's said during the past few months. He's forever chopping and changing his mind about what he means to do with the house and, if I were you, I wouldn't take this latest fad too seriously, until we get it in writing.'

'But it's different this time, Geoffrey. Surely you must see that?'

'On the contrary, I see no difference at all and I'm beginning to wonder if he really knows himself what he's talking about half the time.'

'Then you can't have been paying attention. I do realise that he's changed his mind once or twice in the past, although never about being glad to have us as tenants, incidentally; but it was only because he kept on hoping that, given time, his son would settle down and consent to live here himself. The difference now is that he has been forced to accept that it won't happen simply because he is up against this new young lady the boy has fallen for and hopes to marry. If you'd really been listening, you'd have heard him say that she's the one who's behind this idea of their going to try their luck in Canada and he knows when he's beaten and, what is more, if you ask me, he seemed quite pleased about it.'

'Oh well,' Geoffrey conceded, 'perhaps I didn't quite catch that bit, he does mumble so, but now that you've told me I do see the force of it. A brave man indeed, who would attempt to go against the wishes of the little woman. However, there would still be nothing to stop him giving us notice to quit and then selling the house for some exorbitant price to someone else.'

'I doubt if he would, though. If we're

good tenants, the chances are we'd be good neighbours too. He also knows that you pay the rent on the nail and that, having given your word, you wouldn't then change your mind and let him down. Avril tells me that's a big risk nowadays when you're trying to sell your house.'

'My dear Janet, you and your friend Avril seem to have thrashed this out pretty thoroughly between you, but isn't there something you've overlooked?'

'Oh, lots, I daresay. What in particular?'

'Do we really need to rush in and commit ourselves in this way? Do we, in a word, really want to live in this part of the world at all?'

Janet and Miranda had a great bond in common at that moment, for, short of being asked to uproot herself and board the next plane to Canada, nothing could have been more exacerbating and infuriating than this question. She was so outraged by it that almost for the first time in their marriage she plunged into speech before her mind had been tamed into producing the tactful response.

'I don't believe it, Geoffrey. I just can't believe my ears. You were the one who wanted to come and live here. It was entirely for your sake that we did so and was I consulted about it? No, I was not. You simply marched in one morning after a round of golf and told me that you had decided to retire early and find a house down here. And now, now if you please, two years later, after all the upheaval of moving here, not to mention chasing round the countryside looking for something permanent, you tell me that you've changed your mind.'

'Not at all, I said nothing of the kind. I merely asked whether, having given it a try, you really feel we belong here.'

'As much as anywhere else, I suppose. Don't you?'

'Not particularly. I've nothing against the place, but I can't say I find the local society very stimulating.'

'Well, you haven't given them or yourself much chance, have you? The only time you take a break from your work is to go and spend a night in London. It seems to me that it wouldn't make much difference where we live, so long as you mean to stick to that routine.'

'Which I don't, as it happens. My business in London can more or less take care of itself now. I've fixed myself up with an agent who has one or two reputable publishers in mind he thinks may be interested, so it's just a question of waiting to see who comes up with the best terms and I can safely leave that end of things to him.'

Already keyed up to a high pitch of resentment and self-pity, this complacent attitude was all Janet needed to send her toppling over the edge. She was on the very point of rounding on him and asking in icy tones whether Jennifer would also be able to manage without him in future, when she was assailed by another shock which temporarily rendered her speechless.

She had been pacing about the room in her agitation, plumping up cushions as though her life depended on it, picking things up and putting them down again and had reached the point in her peregrinations where she was pulling some dead heads off the begonia plant in the window and was just in time to see a blue saloon car pull in beside the garden gate.

'Oh, God,' she muttered, 'not him again. I can't stand it.'

'What on earth's the matter now?'

'It's that man, that Superintendent. He's come back.'

'How do you know?' Geoffrey asked,

joining her by the window and sounding rather odd himself.

'I recognise his car. Look, there he is, unlatching the gate. You'll have to let him in yourself. I'm going upstairs to tidy up a bit. I'm sure my face is a wreck and I'm not in the mood to be sociable. Besides, I'm sure it's you he's come to see.'

She had reached the door by the time the bell rang and Tubby, who by then had backed off a few paces so as to give himself a view of the interior, saw her go bounding up the stairs, two steps at a time.

Geoffrey seemed to have been infected by her panic and Janet, skulking in the shadow at the top of the staircase, heard him say, 'Come inside. I assume you're here to tell me the game is up?' and the other voice replying, 'Well, that's really up to you, you know, but I thought you might have something you were ready to tell me,' before they moved away towards the sitting room and out of earshot.

2

'An embittered and disappointed man, in some respects,' Tubby announced when he returned to his office a few hours later.

'I'm sure you're right, sir,' Frank Ross replied obediently, 'although he doesn't seem to have had too bad a life.'

'Oh, quite a creditable and blameless career, of course, but I have the impression he was expecting something altogether more distinguished; set out to climb to the top of the ladder and could never quite make out why it eluded him. Perhaps his dull, correct wife held him back, but I'm inclined to think it was some deficiency in himself. One of those unfortunate souls who, if they ever do step out of line and take a risk, always pick the wrong one.'

'All the same, he might have got away with it this time.'

'He might, yes, and when he turned up here two years ago it must have seemed to him that he really was on to a winner. In his curious, twisted way, he saw himself in the unique position of being able to expose a fraud, thereby righting a great wrong and achieving fame and fortune in the process.'

'So why didn't he bring it off, I wonder?'

'Swimming out of his depth is my guess. When it came to the crunch he misjudged the situation and lost his head. Anyway, that's one side of our story dealt with. How about the blackmail trail? Anything new on that?'

'Not so's you'd notice, but evidence, or rather lack of it suggests that it might still be worth following up, if you think it's necessary.'

'I can't deal with paradoxes so early in the day, Frank. Kindly put it in simpler terms.'

'Thanks to co-operation from North Yorkshire, enquiries were put on foot regarding houses for sale or under offer. Scarborough is a booming place these days and properties are changing hands all the time, through banks and insurance companies and so on, as well as the regular estate agents. They've all been checked out as well as solicitors and banks dealing with probate, and no mention of the name Wicker has yet been found. So, to that extent, anyway, they don't appear to have been telling the truth, but something may still turn up.'

'I see. Incidentally, how much longer have they got in their present job?'

'Another ten days.'

'That's all right, then. They're not likely to step out of line at a time like this, with all eyes watching their every move, so we can allow ourselves to set them aside, at any rate for the time being. If they were in the blackmail game, their source of revenue has certainly dried up now. So what other loose ends to be tidied up before we go into action?'

Frank pushed a newspaper cutting across the desk for his chief's perusal. 'I've just seen this, sir. I think you may find it interesting.'

The cutting, from the *West Sussex Gazette*, was headed 'Young Farmer to Wed' and showed a smiling couple. The man was instantly recognisable as young Rupert Crossman. His intended, smiling happily towards the camera, was not Miranda Jones, but was nevertheless known to both the Superintendent and the Sergeant.

'Yes, I think at last we are getting somewhere,' Tubby said sadly.

Twenty-one

Avril had been hoping to round things off in an artistic fashion by assembling the same guests for lunch on Whit Sunday as had been present at Easter.

Robert got his programme off to a good start by announcing a day or two in advance that he would be spending the weekend on a fishing trip in Scotland with two of his male cronies, but she soon had to face the fact that there would be other absentees as well and in the end she whittled down her list to three, Tubby Wiseman, Billy Jones and Martha.

Rhapsodising over the wine, as tradition required of him, Tubby glanced from one to the other of the faces on either side, amusing himself by trying to assess how far their thoughts diverged from their spoken words. Billy, who had little to say as usual, could, for all anyone knew, be allowing his mind to wander freely over subjects of interest only to himself and totally unconnected with his surroundings. Martha, in her way, was an even harder nut to crack because, although she appeared to be paying close attention to everything the others said, she rarely voiced an opinion of her own and when she did it was delivered in so faltering and apologetic a fashion as to give the impression that she was mentally sub-normal, which he knew to be very wide of the truth.

No such auras of enigma surrounded Avril, whose every utterance exactly reflected whatever thought had just entered her head, one reason, possibly, why Robert spent so much time away from home, and she now lived up to this reputation by saying, 'I'm so glad you approve, Tubby, because I gave of Robert's best this time. I had an ulterior motive, you see.'

'Oh, surely not?'

'I'm afraid so. I was hoping to lull you into telling us what really went on at Uppfield and how you managed to catch that rascal. You know we are all dying to hear.'

'Oh, you mustn't give me the credit for that, Avril. I am only what you'd call the co-ordinator. It's the people who burrow away out of sight and come up with the right answer that we have to thank.'

'So, as they can't do it for themselves, you have a positive duty to do so for them.'

'Only on the strict understanding that I shan't be passing on official secrets, or classified information. It will all be made public in due course.'

'Yes, I'm sure, but it's the due course bit which is so frustrating. One likes to be ahead of the crowd. So when did it all begin?'

'Oh, a long way back. The other thing I should warn you about is that we have to jump around in time quite a lot. In fact, I shall start almost at the end, on Easter Sunday, when we were all seated round this table, just as we are now.'

'Only not all of us are,' Martha pointed out.

'Personally,' Avril said, 'I don't call that anywhere near the end. It was ages before the fire and we hadn't even heard about the spoof corpse then.'

Billy, who had given every indication of having fallen asleep during this altercation, now rouse himself to say, 'If I were you, Avril, I should let him get on and tell it in his own way. You know that he will in the end, however much you interrupt, so it will save time and energy.'

'The reason for starting there,' Tubby said, breaking the silence that followed this advice, 'is that some interesting information came to light concerning the chief character in a series of events following immediately after that Sunday lunch. I refer, of course, to Sam Waddington and, in fact, although he had lived amongst us for eight or ten years, it was the first time any of us had met someone who had known him before he came here. You will recall that there was some difference of opinion concerning his first name and young Mr Gillford, Anthony, I believe he's called, maintained in the face of some opposition, that it was Jim. As it turned out, he was right, but what struck me at the time was the reason he gave for having remembered it. He told us that he had been reading the novel *Lucky Jim* and had found such a strong resemblance between Waddington and the eponymous hero that the name had stayed with him ever since.'

'Goodness me, Tubby, imagine your remembering a trivial little incident like that.'

'In fact, it was far from trivial, Avril, quite the reverse. I'm sure you've read the book yourself, or at any rate heard enough about it to agree that by no stretch of the imagination would those of us who were acquainted with the Waddington of Uppfield, or knew his reputation, have likened him to that particular character. A more remote and unsociable man would have been hard to find.'

'People do tend to change as they get

247

older, you know,' Martha reminded him, sounding rather sad about it.

'To some extent, I agree, but it's mainly in superficial ways. You, for instance, strike me as being pretty much the same woman, underneath a few grey hairs, as you were thirty years ago. However, be that as it may, it seemed to me, after his death, that it was a contradiction which might be worth following up and I was fortunate enough to come across someone else who'd known him in the past. Once again, the description was of a good humoured, happy-go-lucky type, quite unlike the man we all knew as Sam Waddington. The single feature which was common to both and which everyone remembered without any prompting was the scar on the upper part of his face.'

He paused here, to allow the message to sink in and Martha was the first to respond. 'I expect I've misunderstood, but are you . . . could you be trying to tell us that they were two different men?'

'Yes, that's exactly what I'm trying to do.'

'So which was the real Waddington?' Avril asked, 'Lucky Jim, or Dismal Sam?'

'Oh, the former, of course, the one who was killed in the car crash. That was another incident which aroused my curiosity right from the start, this apparent confusion as to whether it was actually Waddington or his companion who had been killed. The answer, in a sense, was both. The genuine Waddington died and the impostor Waddington lived on to impersonate him and, in due course, inherit Uppfield and all that went with it.'

'Were you able to find any proof of that?' Avril asked.

'Enough for immediate purposes. Legal proof may take months, perhaps years to establish, but, thanks to information from one of our fellow guests on Easter Day, we are in no doubt as to the identity of the false Waddington, that is, the man who survived the accident and switched passport, papers and clothing with his dead companion. Of course, there are parts of the story we shall never know, since he too is now dead. One, for instance, is whether he deliberately slashed his own face, so that it would be permanently scarred, or whether his injuries were such as to put the idea of impersonation into his head in the first place.'

'And since, as you say, he is now dead, I suppose all this was of academic interest only,' Billy suggested.

'I take your meaning, of course, but I don't agree with it. We still had a murderer on our hands, who was very much alive and we had a better chance of catching up with him if we knew what his motive was, and that was likely to depend, to a large extent, on the history and personality of his victim. One thing we noticed, for instance, was that the false Waddington, either through guilt or fear of being exposed as a fraud, had become daily more unlike the original one. As you know, he virtually cut himself off from the neighbours and I daresay he was haunted by the idea that one of them might turn out to have known his so-called father quite well, could even have heard tales about the youthful Waddington, or seen photographs of him as a boy. Such friends as he did invite came either from London, or, in some cases, America, all of them comparatively young and with memories that did not go far enough back to make them potentially dangerous.

'It was a similar story with the domestic staff. Not one of them lived in the house, you'll remember. The nearest anyone came to that was the couple at the Lodge and they too, as the paranoia mounted, got their marching orders, for reasons, which if not fabricated, were later found to have been greatly exaggerated. It seemed a solid enough premise on which to base our campaign. Unfortunately, however, as so often happens, it led to a false trail.'

'Oh, what a shame,' Avril said. 'And what an anti-climax after all that build-up. What was wrong about it?'

'As it turned out, he was a marked man, in any case. It was his own character which sowed the seeds of hatred and revenge and brought about his death and the fact that he was travelling under a false name had nothing to do with it.'

'Except, perhaps . . . that is, if I haven't got the wrong end of the stick, you could say that it was all the deceit and trickery which turned him into the character he became, so to that extent you were on the right track, after all?'

'Thank you, Martha, I appreciate those words of comfort.'

'What I'd like to know,' Avril said, 'is how you found out who he really was and what he was doing before he turned up here as Sam Waddington.'

'And I shall be happy to tell you because it follows from what I said earlier about the way he cut himself off from his own generation, particularly those of them from around here. Ironically enough, it was the exception he made to that rule which brought about his downfall.'

'Oh, this sounds better. Do explain.'

'The summer before last a gentleman who prefers to remain anonymous was staying at a rented cottage about fifteen miles from here. One morning he was invited to play a round of golf and afterwards, in the clubhouse, a man named Sam Waddington was pointed out to him, along with a summary of his eventful life and the fact that he had inherited a vast property and sacks of money from his father, whom he hadn't set eyes on for over twenty years. Our man, who in the best tradition I shall henceforth refer to as Mr X, was interested to hear this, having known someone of that name himself during his sojourn in the Far East and even more interested that this one bore small resemblance to the other, except in one very noticeable feature. He too had a long diagonal scar across his forehead. Most interesting of all, however, was that the man at the golf club, probably by some small gesture or mannerism, brought back vivid memories to Mr X of a fellow pupil he had come to know well during their last year at school, but had not seen again, except on one occasion in their early twenties, when they had both attended a Memorial Service for their former headmaster. This comparatively minor episode made such an impression on Mr X that it radically changed the course of his life.'

'How very dramatic,' Avril said. 'I know I ought not to keep interrupting, but how on earth could it have done that?'

'In order to explain, I must now tell you something of the background of Mr X. He was in his late fifties at the time I am speaking of and coming to the end of a long and blameless, but unspectacular career, most of it spent overseas. He had done a respectable job, but he had never touched the heights. Various attempts to break out of the mould of mediocrity had failed and to that extent he was a disappointed man. Now those past failures and this new and tantalising discovery came together to provide him with a purpose in life. He decided then and there to retire, to settle down somewhere within easy reach of the golf club, so as to be able to monitor the activities of his quarry and to devote himself to writing a best-selling blockbuster of a novel.'

The reaction to this news being all that

he could have asked for, Tubby paused for a moment to allow it to sink in before saying, 'A trifle optimistic, you may be saying to yourselves, but you must make allowances for the fact that he is someone who had always seen himself as destined for success and only the opportunity had so far eluded him. Also, to be fair, he had got himself into the hands of a character, one Spencer Worthington, who is a literary agent of sorts and who was busily fanning these flames of grandeur, with much talk of film rights and American markets.'

'Do you mean a crime novel?' Billy asked. 'Sort of *Mysterious Affair at Uppfield*, for instance?'

'No, nothing like that, just a straightforward account of two separate men, who ended up as one who lived out his declining years on a vast estate, with a vast income, which, to all intents and purposes, were stolen property. And the real joy of it was that he could stick as close to the truth as he liked, without the slightest chance of being sued for libel. Unfortunately, however, after six months of plodding away in solitude, he began, as so many writers do, I am reliably informed, to go slightly mad.'

'Did he really?' Avril asked. 'You do surprise me. I have always found him such a dull man, but no less sane than most. Still, I'm not really supposed to know who he is, am I? So perhaps you'd better strike those comments from the Minutes. What form did his madness take? Not making straw effigies and sticking knives into them, by any chance?'

'No, that was the work of someone else. Our Mr X became so obsessed by this project of his that eventually he could no longer resist the temptation to share the secret with someone else and that someone turned out to be the victim, no less. Waddington received at least one letter from him, and there are likely to have been more, in which Mr X described exactly what he was up to. Furthermore, they were written in a code, which he and half a dozen school fellows had invented as their private language. Waddington had no idea which one it was and hadn't to the best of his knowledge, set eyes on any of them for thirty years or more, had probably forgotten most of their names by that time. But the letters made it clear that his persecutor was living close by, keeping him under observation and intended to continue doing so.'

At this point Tubby broke off the narrative in order to refill his glass from the decanter, which Avril had thoughtfully placed by his right hand. It was a minute or two before he resumed and, in doing so, he adopted a lighter and more conversational tone, rather in the style of a schoolmaster, who at the conclusion of the lesson spends an extra ten minutes on informal discussion.

'I am sure you must all be wondering why I have kept you waiting so long, taking you through all these preliminaries. It was necessary, though, in order for you to understand that from the day that Mr X arrived on the scene Waddington's game was up. Soon afterwards it began to dawn on him too and he saw that his only escape from these terrible clutches was to dispose of his property on the most favourable terms he could contrive and remove himself to another part of the globe, where his tormentor could never find him. Unfortunately though, even in such extremities as these, the leopard does not change its spots and these favourable terms were an important element in his plan. That's why he made the deal with the consortium who were offering to buy him out and re-develop the land. And then he had what he considered to be a further stroke of luck. He met and fell in love with a young woman who seemed to reciprocate his feelings. What better way to start a new life than with a wife who would not only take care of him but provide him with a certain camouflage. He took care to keep the details of his marriage a secret from the locals but the truth is that when he signed his marriage certificate he also, as the saying goes, signed his own death warrant because his new wife Susannah, as you all now know, was none other than the Annie who had jilted Rupert Crossman a few months earlier.'

'A very shocking state of affairs,' Avril said, sounding far from shocked. 'I couldn't be more delighted that he got his just desserts. Can't help feeling sorry for Miranda, though. Is she very badly put out, Billy?'

'Naturally, she is, who wouldn't be? She has been callously exploited by that young man, and no mistake. Far from catching him on the rebound after his broken engagement it was he who was using her as cover for his nefarious purposes. I am glad to say that fortunately she wasn't in love with him long enough for the scars to be very deep.'

'Do you mean she'd begun to cool off

even before she knew the truth about everything?' Martha asked.

'Well, to be honest, it's hard to say which came first. Looking back on it, it seems that in some curious way, the two things came about simultaneously. She seems to have become disenchanted with Rupert at the very same moment as she began to scent something menacing behind his father's obsessive hatred of Waddington. I can't say whether it was a logical, or even conscious connection, but she certainly became seriously worried about the subject of heredity, though I believe she was as surprised as the rest of us when we heard that it was Crossman senior who had been arrested on a murder charge. You see, she had become convinced that it was Rupert who had done the deed, and what is more, she thought Rupert was aware of her suspicions and was pressing the marriage as a way of keeping her quiet. Yet she loved him and pitied him too. One can only be thankful that Tubby's men got there before the wedding and not after.'

'Let's drink to that,' Avril said. 'It makes one feel quite sick to think what might have become of her, if she had gone through with it. Imagine using his own father, who was so devoted to him, as a tool in his own wicked schemes.'

'Did he do that?' Martha asked. 'I had no idea. In what way did he use him?'

'Tubby will explain.'

'No doubt about it,' Tubby said, seizing the chance to do so. 'Rupert is a very cool customer who was willing to use any tool at his disposal to achieve his aims. And his aims largely centred on greed and the ambition to possess more than the modest wealth his father would eventually leave him. And being lazy, he had no desire to work for this wealth, and being impatient he wanted it at once. The piece of land that his father had lost to Waddington rankled deeply and the feud that followed made him aware of the rising land values in this area. He paid lip service to his father's ideas on preserving the countryside but his unscientific farming methods which lost a quarter of the profits irritated him deeply. And then he had several strokes of luck. He met Susannah Lennard, who was called Annie by her friends, and fell in love with her. It was a case of like meeting like. She was already comfortably off through her divorce settlement and was not averse to acquiring more wealth. They became engaged. And Crossman, the poor fool, was so happy he went straight out and bought them a house a few miles down the road from his own. In the meantime, however, Annie had taken Rupert on several occasions to stay with a girl friend and her husband who had often spent weekends as guests at Uppfield Court. You may imagine their pleasure and astonishment to discover that it was only a few miles from Rupert and Annie's future home and they insisted that they should all get together next time they came down. And so it was that in due course their names were added to the list of young people Waddington liked to have about him.'

'But surely he must have known who Rupert was?' Martha objected.

'I daresay he did, but I don't suppose it bothered him. He must have imagined that the feud had ended with the court case and did not involve young Rupert. Maybe he imagined that his hospitality could compensate for the Crossmans' loss. He also knew enough about James Crossman to be quite sure that they hadn't been at school together and that was really beginning to be his only yardstick, so far as other people were concerned.'

'I do believe you're right,' Billy said,

coming to life again. 'I remember that a year or so ago, just after I started working on conversion plans for the house, Waddington put me through an inquisition on my educational background, which school, which university and so on. It was rather puzzling, but I concluded that he had begun to have doubts about my credentials to practise as an architect. Anyway, he seemed satisfied with the answers and the subject was never referred to again. I had forgotten all about it till this minute.'

'What I find harder to understand,' Avril said, 'is how Rupert got away with it.'

'With what?'

'These secret visits to Uppfield. If his father was really such a gorgon, surely he would have wanted to know where his son was spending his weekends. It must have been quite a strain inventing lies to put him off the scent?'

'He didn't need to invent anything. As far as his father was concerned he was spending his weekends with his fiancée's family in London. And then a dreadful thing happened. Waddington fell in love with Annie. At first the two young people laughed about the old man's infatuation. But he persisted; flowers, dinners, expensive trinkets—and at some point, we don't know when, everything changed.'

Tubby paused to refill his glass, satisfied that his audience was hanging on his every word. He would have been less than human if he'd resisted the dramatic potential of his narrative, and Tubby would have been the first to admit that he was more human than most. He lowered his voice and attempted to look conspiratorial. 'What I am about to tell you will never prove in a court of law. We have no evidence except a newspaper cutting, a photograph and a pair of spectacles with plain glass lenses and that is not sufficient to prove a charge of conspiracy. But what next took place probably runs like this. We don't know which of them had the idea first, Rupert or the girl—I would like to think it was the girl because . . . well, anyway, whoever it was, they decided that Annie should encourage Sam Waddington's attentions, publicly ditch Rupert and marry Waddington instead. The plan was for Waddington to meet an untimely death shortly after the wedding, probably by arranging some suitable riding accident or mock burglary. It is a remarkable feature in this case that all Waddington's insurance policies were substantially increased after the wedding, as if he had in some way anticipated his own death. This was all the work of the careful widow-to-be.'

Tubby drew breath and looked round. Billy was very pale indeed. Tubby hurried on with his story. 'While Annie was busying herself with these matters, Rupert's role was to fortify his local links and distance himself from Uppfield and Annie. In pursuing these ends he threw himself vociferously into the anti-development lobby, much to his father's delight and, I am extremely sorry to say, began courting a local girl whom we all know and like and who, I must say, deserves far better.' He looked round fiercely, as if challenging contradiction.

'Then things started to go wrong. The first hitch was that Miranda began suspecting him of being involved in the stabbed dummy caper. I have yet to gather evidence as to how this came about but, be that as it may, the suspicion was there and Rupert knew it. But there was worse to come, for Rupert's father found out that Waddington had married Annie. Not knowing the ins and outs of the matter, he was devastated on his son's behalf. He felt that Waddington was out to destroy his family, grabbing not only money, land and a way of life, but now a bride and thus potentially children, a future generation. This finally pushed Crossman over the edge and turned him from a relatively harmless eccentric into a raving lunatic.'

'He looked sane enough when I last saw him,' Avril chipped in. 'He was at a Council meeting on the Tuesday after the fire at Uppfield and he made some extremely sensible contributions.'

'I believe most psychiatrists would agree with you, that madness can wear many sane disguises,' Tubby replied. 'But I think you will find that poor Crossman will be found unfit to plead when the time comes for his trial. Far from wanting Rupert to stay in the district and inherit the farm, he was now encouraging him to emigrate, to start a new life in Canada, away from Uppfield and the evil power of Waddington. And then the final blow fell. On the Saturday before the fire he overheard a telephone conversation between his son and his son's ex-fiancée, now Mrs Waddington, which made their continuing relationship clear to him and also revealed their plans. The role played by extension telephones in this case is quite remarkable,' Tubby mused, looking at Martha thoughtfully.

'Anyway,' he continued, 'Annie Wad-dington informed Rupert that Sam pro-posed to spend a few days at Uppfield on his own and the time had therefore come to put the final part of their plan into opera-tion.'

Tubby surveyed his audience severely. 'Please let none of you forget that all I am now saying is hypothesis and will probably never be proved. It is bad enough that the villain of the piece is allowed to roam the world free for want of evidence to convict, without me ending up in court, fighting my way out of a libel case.'

Avril and Martha nodded enthusiasti-cally; Billy appeared to have fallen asleep again. Tubby resumed his hypothesis.

'Whatever plan was outlined on the tele-phone, old Crossman was absolutely hor-rified. Yes, he hated Waddington—but murder? But then perhaps it was he who was responsible . . . After all, his obsessive feud with Waddington had dominated young Rupert's boyhood. Now it was about to turn him into a murderer. No, it must not be allowed to happen, he must at least save his son from that. He spent a sleepless night and wandered through the Downs the following day. Very early the next day,

Monday, he went up to Uppfield and rang the doorbell. Waddington himself, still in his pyjamas, let him in, probably somewhat astonished by this early call from an old enemy. Crossman allowed him no time to speculate about the purpose of the call but biffed him smartly on the jaw and knocked him out. There is no need for you to wonder how I know all this,' Tubby intercepted Martha's look of growing scepticism. 'This part is taken from Crossman's detailed statement after his arrest. Anyway, after that, he carried Waddington upstairs and put him back into his bed. Then he laid a neat fire at the foot of the stairs, lit it with the aid of some paraffin from the toolshed and a cigar butt from an ashtray and took his leave. And, according to him, once he had done all this, it was as if a great load had been lifted from him, he could breathe, he felt free.'

Tubby completed his narrative and silence followed. Then Avril said, 'Well, I suppose we should congratulate you and I do, of course, but I can't help feeling sorry for the poor old fool. What do you suppose will happen to Rupert and Annie?'

'They were already on the other side of the Atlantic by the time the balloon went up. They are rich beyond their wildest dreams but I do not suppose that wealth thus acquired will bring them much joy. It brought little enough to Sam Waddington.'

Other aspects of the case were exercising Billy's mind. 'What interests me more than that is something you were saying earlier about Mr X and his dreams of becoming a best-selling novelist. Didn't even Mrs X guess what he was up to?'

'She realised he was deceiving her, but, being a somewhat naïve and unimaginative sort of woman, she equated that with one thing only, the Other Woman. Mind you, she had some excuse. Our Mr X is a rather parsimonious man and when he discovered that his first wife was back in London and all set to pick it up where they had left off, he did not scruple to fall in with the idea and thus provide himself with free board and lodging. It didn't last, though. She soon began to want more from him than the occasional bunch of flowers and he had no intention of abandoning his comfortable, well-run home and comfortable, well-trained wife for an adventure of that kind.'

'Which accounts for a lot, don't you think? And how fascinating to discover how little some married couples know about each other,' Avril remarked, toying with a spoon, as though debating whether to use it as a gavel. 'Any more questions before we adjourn for coffee?'

'I have one,' Martha said, astonishing everyone. 'That is, it doesn't really have much significance, just curiosity more than anything, but did you ever discover, Tubby, what that man, Wicker, was doing at Uppfield during the Easter holiday? I hope you won't mind my asking?'

'Far from minding, Martha, I am glad you have asked.'

'Oh, really? Why is that?'

'Because I am bound to confess that it did cross my mind that your story of his driving up from the house to the Lodge might have been due to some sort of trick of the light, let's say; or even, as has been known, some sort of attempt to put me off whatever scent I might be following.'

Martha listened to this in silence and with a grave and attentive expression, but a slight flush had crept over her horsey, angular features and he still could not be certain whether she was out-bluffing him or not.

He could easily have shaken her, but, at the same time, not being one to spurn the smallest of silver linings, told himself that it would be salutary to remember, if he were ever to become complacent in his dealings with the criminal classes, that Martha was just as much of an unknown quantity to him now as she had been when he first met her all those years ago.